THE SECOND ROOM

BY

CHARO STECUM

TSR

The moments we leave behind and the ones that wait for us anyway.

Chapter One

ROOM KEY

Sienna Hartley had done her time in hotel rooms. From brutalist budget boxes in Berlin, to five-star French castles with beds that swallowed you whole. This time, she was in her hometown, New York, and the lobby smelled like roses and money.

She pulled her suitcase behind her, the wheels clacking over polished marble that gleamed with the kind of cleanliness only found in places with full-time staff. She hated conferences. She hated forced small talk, corporate hashtags, and overpriced hotel wine. But more than anything, she hated the version of herself she had to perform at them; the shiny, agreeable Sienna who smiled through presentations and made mental notes on how many people commented on her age.

This one, however, felt like a misstep. The lighting was too ambient, the welcome from the doorman too chirpy, and this hotel was full of rich strangers.

"Checking in. Sienna Hartley. Should be under Sapphire Creative."
The concierge, Harper, was young, too dewy, and smiled like she'd been trained in a lab.

"Of course, Ms Hartley. Welcome to Deliciae."
"Thanks. Do you have a room without a view of other people's regrets?"

The girl giggled and typed faster.

As she waited, Sienna scanned the lobby. Velvet lounges. Crystal light fixtures. A pianist in the corner was playing something tasteful and sad. The whole place screamed luxury, and she'd kill for room service and six hours of not being perceived.

"Here's your key. Room 408. Your suite is part of a dual configuration, an architectural layout quirk. You and Room 409 share access to a private lounge between the suites. It's completely separate from the main hotel areas."

Sienna wanted to scream at the thought of sharing a private lounge; sharing wasn't private at all. Instead, she took the key card, thanked the concierge, adjusted her coat, and walked toward the lifts. As the doors slid shut behind her, she exhaled the kind of sigh that said: get through this and then go home and rebuild your life.

⚷
TSR

Upstairs, the hallway was silent. Plush carpet, dim wall sconces, moody glamour. Room 408 greeted her with a soft beep as she slid in the key card. The suite was enormous. Too enormous for one. A seating area, bar cart, and velvet armchair by the window. She flung her heels off and padded barefoot across the room, opening the mini fridge for sparkling water and already plotting how she could fake a migraine and skip tomorrow's keynote.

Now, alone in Room 408, she peeled off her coat and surveyed the damage. The room was immaculate. Cool-toned. Luxe, in that too-considered way. Velvet pillows, chrome fixtures, a minibar stocked for

Instagram. She padded toward the adjoining door.

It was shut. Good. She didn't want company. Not from Room 409.

Not from her inbox. Not from Olivia, who had already messaged twice:

"You checked in? Want to grab a drink at the bar before the welcome session?
Or are you already hiding from the world with minibar whiskey?"

Sienna didn't respond. She tossed her phone face down on the bench, unzipped her suitcase with one finger, and pulled out the robe. Her own instead of the hotel one. Slate-grey silk, embroidered initials. A gift to herself the day she signed the divorce papers. One of many.

The conference didn't start until tomorrow. Tonight was technically optional. That's how she justified skipping it entirely.

Her phone buzzed again. Olivia, this time with a voice message:

"At the bar. Sitting next to someone from Fonts and Strategy who talks in hashtags. SOS."

Sienna chuckled but didn't reply. She stepped into the lounge to test the waters, modern mid-century furniture, a low marble table, moody lighting, and a complimentary cheese board between two carafes of water. The second door, Room 409, was closed. She exhaled and poured herself a glass of red.

Then she heard it. A soft thump.

She froze. It had come from the lounge door connecting to the next suite.

Another sound. Movement.

She walked over and pressed her ear against it. Low jazz. The scrape of a chair.

Then - click. Panic.

She jumped back, perched casually on one of the chairs, trying to look like she hadn't just been eavesdropping.

The door opened, and standing there, barefoot, in a charcoal T-shirt
and grey sweatpants, holding a book and a wine glass, was a man.

He looked up. Paused. Then smiled. "You must be 408."

Sienna blinked. "And you must be... not room service."

He laughed, warm and low. "Nico. 409. They told me there was a
lounge. Didn't realise it meant I'd have a neighbour through a door."

She took him in. Early fifties, maybe. Salt-and-pepper chocolate hair,
slight stubble, captivating eyes, too steady for someone casually
drinking alone. Gorgeous, in the kind of way that made her forget she
was supposed to be unimpressed.

"Well," she said, "as long as you don't snore through walls or play the
trumpet at midnight, we'll get along."

He raised the glass. "Noted."

She gave a polite smile. "I should probably go settle in properly."

"Of course," he said, still holding his glass.

She closed her door gently. Then hovered there, heartbeat just a little
faster.

She didn't know why.

She unpacked. Silk blouse. Laptop. A copy of a book she wasn't going
to read. In the bathroom, she wiped away the city with micellar water
and caught her own reflection. Her reflection was sharp-featured and
striking, a face more sculpted than soft, framed by shoulder-length
blonde hair that had once been sun-kissed, now professionally
highlighted. Her eyes were deep blue, with lashes as long as the Nile, set
wide apart under perfectly arched brows. Elegant, some would say. Icy,
others. She had the kind of beauty that intimidated receptionists and
made ex-boyfriends apologise for years.

She curled up in the armchair with her phone. She scrolled past photos
of smiling colleagues already posting from the hotel bar. The thought

of smiling for another camera made her physically recoil.

She got up, wandered the suite. Paused at the window and took in the soft sprawl of city lights beneath her. It was quieter than she'd expected. A little too quiet for the mind of a woman who had spent the last year trying to rewrite her life from scratch.

She opened the wardrobe, half-expecting the bathrobe to still have its tag. Instead, she found a plush black velvet hanger that reminded her of Paris. A city she once loved before it became a backdrop for someone else's engagement. She shook the thought off.

A soft knock sounded; it wasn't from the main door; it was from the lounge.

Nico's voice, gentle: "I promise I'm not a weirdo. But I've got a bottle of red and a cheese board I'll never finish alone. In case you'd rather eat than scroll."

She hesitated. Every instinct said no. Every instinct also remembered she hadn't eaten since breakfast.

Sienna opened the lounge door.

"Fine. But only because I'm hungry. And if you're a serial killer, I'm not that easy to kill."

He smiled, stepping aside. "I like your odds."

The shared lounge was softly lit, a low couch facing a record player, the table transformed with wine, bread, cheese, and candles, actual candles.

Sienna sat, folding one leg under her. "This is... unexpectedly charming."

"I'm full of surprises," Nico said, pouring her a glass. "To new neighbours."

She clinked his glass. Candlelight flickered between them, painting his face in gold and shadow.

"So," he said, "what brings you to Deliciae? Please don't say soul-searching."

She smirked. "Conference. Branding and creative direction. I'll be sitting in a ballroom tomorrow pretending I care about fonts and slogans while smiling at keynote speakers and dying inside."

"Sounds cutthroat." He replied.

"Only if someone dares say, 'authenticity is our brand' with a straight face."

He laughed again, easy, rich. She found herself watching his mouth, his lips, then immediately hated that she noticed.

He topped up her wine. "And what do you do when you're not silently judging?"

"I create campaigns for other people to silently judge."

"Ah. A beautiful contradiction."

Their eyes met, and there was a long pause. Then he looked away first; he was calm. Like he was used to letting women look as long as they liked.

Sienna tore a piece of bread. "And you? Local or passing through mysterious-loner style?"

"Neither. I'm in town for time off. I take photos. War zones, protests, pandemics. Now mostly private commissions."

"So, you traded trauma for boutique hotels?"

"Something like that."

She wasn't sure if it was the wine, or the lighting, or the way he listened, but she felt warmer than expected. It had been a long time since someone looked at her and saw more than the surface.

She glanced toward the door. She didn't want to leave; she couldn't remember the last time she'd stayed.

"I should probably go," she said eventually.

"Of course," he replied.

"Thanks for the cheese. And the... unexpected company."

"Anytime."

She stepped back into her room, half-finished wine in hand. She closed her door, then, without meaning to, left it just slightly open.

And this time, not out of politeness.

Out of possibility.

Chapter Two

NIGHT LIGHT

Sienna blinked awake to the sound of her phone buzzing against the marble-topped nightstand. The curtains were drawn, but the light behind them was loud. She groaned, reached out, and checked the time, 9:47 a.m.

Three messages from Olivia. One from a client. One marked URGENT from Marc. She turned the volume off and dropped the phone onto the bed.

Last night had been... unexpected. The wine. The candles. Nico. His voice still lingered in her head, low, calm, with that slightly amused tone of someone who doesn't need to try.

She padded barefoot to the bathroom, splashed her face, and tied her robe with a sharp tug. She wasn't hungover, but she felt emotionally puffy. Her thoughts were still lounging in the candlelight, half-dressed and sentimental. Then, three soft knocks.

The lounge door.
She didn't realise she had left it ajar; she opened it slowly.
Nico was there, this time in a rolled-up button-down, holding two takeaway coffees and a paper bag that smelled like butter and sin all rolled into one.

"Peace offering," he said, lifting them slightly. "For the uninvited cheese board."

She looked at him, then down at herself—bare legs, robe, yesterday's mascara haunting her.

"I'm not exactly dressed for diplomacy."

He tilted his head toward the lounge. "Join me in neutral territory? There's pastry. And plausible deniability."

She smirked. "Only if it's real coffee and not brown water in a cup."

"I'll let you be the judge," he said.

The shared lounge looked different in daylight, less seductive, more sincere. The candles were gone, but the warmth lingered.

They sat across from each other, coffees in hand, croissants flaking between them like snow.

"So," she said, tearing a corner. "You don't seem like the conference type."

"I'm not." He sipped. "Are you?"

"Tragically, yes. Though I'm technically on leave."

"Ah. So, this is... what? Voluntary torture?"

She sighed. "Marc, my ex and former business partner, insisted I 'show face.' Strategic optics, he said. I told him to shove his optics. Then I showed up anyway."

Nico raised his cup. "To boundaries we still haven't learned to enforce."

Her phone buzzed again. Olivia.

"Are you alive? Are you trapped under something heavy? You're on the printed agenda, FYI.

If I have to suffer alone through the 'Brand Authenticity' panel, I will burn this place down."

Sienna shook her head and smiled. She stretched.

"I have to go."

"To branding?" he asked.

"To theatre," she muttered.

She paused at the doorway to her room, hand brushing the frame. The robe shifted against her skin like a reminder of softness, of hesitation, of everything she didn't usually let anyone see. She glanced back at Nico, still seated.

My god, she thought, he really is gorgeous. Annoyingly so. The kind of gorgeous that made you want to roll your eyes and check for a wedding ring, or worse, a personality cult. She'd have to be careful not to let her jaw drop. She knew better. But apparently, wisdom had its limits.

She slipped inside to get dressed, grabbed her bag, and looked in the mirror, steadying herself for whatever version of her the day expected.

TSR

Downstairs, the conference was already in full swing. Branded lanyards, stiff blazers, teeth too white for the lighting. Sienna slid into a seat beside Olivia, who passed her a coffee from the communal urn as if it were contraband.

"Late night?" Olivia whispered.

"Cheese charm."

Olivia arched a brow. "You're glowing."

"Stop."

They sat through a keynote on audience personas delivered by a man who used the phrase "likeability matrix" and didn't bat an eye.

Olivia texted from beside her:

"He just said 'synergy' unironically. Send help."

Olivia scrolled through her phone again, frowning at something she didn't share.

"Crisis?" Sienna asked.

"Opportunity," Olivia said, still frowning. "I just haven't decided if I'm the type who takes them anymore."

Sienna raised a brow. "Since when do you hesitate?"

"Since I started thinking before acting," Olivia said. "It's wildly overrated."

Sienna stifled a laugh, then zoned out completely. Her mind wandered back to the lounge. Nico's voice. The way he watched her, not like he wanted to take something, but like he noticed something already his.

By late afternoon, she was done. Socially. Mentally. Existentially.

She made her escape, took the lift, and let herself into her suite with a deep, theatrical sigh.

The blazer came off first. Then the shoes. She unclipped her earrings like they were handcuffs. Her phone rang.

Marc.

She stared at it. Let it ring. Then picked it up.

"What?"

"That's quite a tone for someone still representing the agency."

"I'm not. I'm on leave. Remember? That thing people take when they're sick of pretending to be fine?"

Marc's voice was smooth, like old glass. "This isn't personal. It's about the pitch. You built Sapphire. Don't let it go slack."

She walked toward the lounge doorway without realising it.

Her voice lifted.

"You're not worried about the agency. You're worried about losing control of the thing you tied to your ego."

A pause. Then the gut punch.

"You sound emotional."

She laughed, sharply but clean. "I sound done. There's a difference."

She hung up.

And that's when she noticed Nico. Standing near the record player. Holding a glass of red. Again.

"I wasn't eavesdropping," he said gently.

She closed her eyes. "That's twice now."

"Bad habit. Standing still."

She exhaled and entered, sinking into the corner chair. "Sorry you had to hear that."

"I didn't mind," he said, topping up her water like it was nothing. "Sometimes it helps to hear yourself say the thing out loud."

She looked at him, suddenly too tired to keep up appearances.

"I used to be the woman who ran the room. Who got in first, got out clean, and didn't explain herself. Now I'm... that woman. The cautionary tale in a good blazer."

Nico leaned against the table. "That's not what I see."

She looked at him. "Then what do you see?"

"A woman who's showing up."

He lifted his glass.

"To bad habits."

She lifted hers.

"To soft landings."

They drank.

And this time, the lounge door didn't just stay open. It stayed inviting.

But eventually, the wine ran out, and the air thickened. Sienna, restless and rattled in a way she couldn't name, needed air, or noise or distance, she wasn't really sure which.

She hadn't meant to leave the room again. But hours later, still wired from the call, from Nico's words, from her own inability to sit still, she found herself walking through the hotel's main hall.

The bar was tucked behind frosted glass and half-curtains, designed for discretion and deep pockets. It was dim, glowing amber from wall lights and a single candelabra on the piano. Someone was playing. A woman in a tuxedo jacket, fingers gliding over the keys like she had nowhere else to be.

Nico. Seated near the end of the bar. Alone. A glass of red in front of him. He didn't see her at first.

Sienna hovered just outside the frame of it all. For once, not needing to be seen. She was... watching.

He looked up.

Met her eyes.

No smile or surprise, a calm curiosity. Like he already knew she'd find him again.

She walked over, heels soft against the carpet, and slid onto the stool beside him.

"I'm not stalking you," she murmured.

"Then I must be hallucinating."

She glanced toward the piano. "She's good."

"She is."

She turned her glass slowly on the bar top.

"I don't usually do this."
"Drink wine in expensive hotels?"
"Talk twice to the same man."
He smiled, and she turned to him.
"There's something about you… I can't place it."
He didn't look away. "That's alright. Some things take time."
Her breath caught briefly. Something in the way he said it, measured, like he already knew the answer to a question she hadn't asked, like he knew her.
She studied him.
The salt-and-pepper stubble. The unhurried posture. The scent of vanilla, amber and bergamot, like warmth tucked beneath expensive fabric.
The way his sleeve brushed her arm when he reached for his glass was casual, but it left her skin aware.
She should've asked where he was from. Or what he did, exactly. Or why everything about him made her feel like she'd been here before.

"That's a dangerously poetic thing to say to a woman who just left a man for calling her difficult."
He smiled at that. "Then I'm in trouble."
She didn't smile. But something in her chest pulled tighter.
There was something about him. Something not quite new.

The pianist slipped into a low, wandering melody, each note dipping like a secret. Sienna could feel herself leaning in, imperceptibly. She wasn't being intentional; it was gravity.
She cleared her throat. "This place makes it easy to forget the outside exists."
Nico tilted his head. "That's the idea."

"And dangerously effective," she added, tracing a drop of condensation on her glass. "You could disappear here if you wanted."

"Maybe that's why we're both here."

That landed.

A pause stretched, warm, charged, not quite still.

She looked at him again, slower this time, and thought - *Do I know you?*

She raised her glass. "To forgetting."

He raised his. "To remembering anyway."

Their glasses touched. The heat from his hand hovered near hers, like something undecided. And for a few suspended seconds, the hotel, the conference, the noise of her life all faded.

There was only this.

Two people. A shared stillness. A second room.

Chapter Three

FAMILIAR STRANGERS

She dreamt of water.

She was standing at the edge of the ocean. The light was all wrong, too bright and too white. The kind that burns before it warms.

Waves rolled in slow motion, folding over themselves without sound. She could hear crying but couldn't find the source. Then the corridor appeared, narrow, long, lined with open doors and empty beds.

The floor was wet. Her feet were bare. Her hands ached to hold something she couldn't name.

At the end of the hall, Nico stood with a camera.

Everything was dark, endless, and oddly still, until the sound of a shutter cut through it. Then Nico's voice. Low, familiar. "Look at me," he said. Saying her name, but not quite. Saying someone's name.

She tried. But her reflection stepped forward instead.

She woke with a start, heart knocking against her ribs like it had somewhere better to be. The room was dim. Outside the drawn curtains, Manhattan moved. Somewhere below: car horns, sirens, someone shouting for a cab. Sienna sat up, pushing hair off her forehead, skin still warm from the dream.

What time was it?

She didn't check.

Instead, she moved through the suite like a ghost still trying to decide whether it wanted to haunt anyone. Shower. Coffee. Black dress.

Leather ankle boots that could crush doubt underfoot. She barely touched the breakfast she'd ordered. Her appetite had become a casualty of proximity.

She stared at the half-eaten toast like it might give her answers. How long had it been since someone's presence, not their demands, not their needs, but their *presence*, had unsettled her like this?
With Marc, she'd always been two steps ahead. With most men, she could see the endings before they began. But with Nico, everything was blurred at the edges.
A stillness pervaded the atmosphere.

She caught herself adjusting her dress in the mirror, then stopped.
You don't need to impress him, she told her reflection.
But she wasn't so sure that's what this was. Maybe she didn't want to impress him. Maybe she wanted to remember something that didn't quite belong to her yet.

Today was the main event. Panels, presentations, branding breakdowns. Sienna told herself she was here for the content. For the agency. For optics. Not because she half-expected to see a familiar face in a sea of strangers. Nico had said he wasn't part of it, but her gaze still drifted, uninvited, scanning for something she couldn't name.
The ballroom buzzed with energy, moss walls, moody lighting, and a screen the size of a small apartment. Olivia was already there, wedged between a barista cart and a conversation about 'disruption pathways.'

The smell of burnt milk and ambition hung in the air. People in groups, in expensive suits, with tone-on-tone lanyards, and exaggerated gestures. Every conversation seemed perfectly rehearsed. Like they were all auditioning for relevance.
Sienna caught glimpses of familiar faces, clients, rivals, that woman

from LA who once pitched her own agency as a "creative mother lode." She wanted to feel something. Excitement. Inspiration. But mostly she felt like a spectator at her own funeral.

"Praise be," Olivia muttered as Sienna slid into the seat beside her. "I thought I was going to have to network without supervision."
"I'm not in a supervising mood," Sienna replied, trying not to grin at Olivia's random one liners and sipping the conference coffee with a grimace.
"This is the Hunger Games of branding conferences," Olivia added, passing her a protein bar like it was a peace offering. "Eat. You look like you've had dreams. And not the sexy kind."
Sienna didn't answer. She unwrapped the bar, took a bite, and tried to look engaged.
She scanned the crowd absently. A man in a taupe jacket was bragging about an empathy-to-ROI ratio. Another was handing out branded mints with QR codes on them.

Somewhere beneath it all, the pull returned, and it had nothing to do with the stage or the job. It was toward the question that had taken human form and wandered into the joint lounge two days ago.

The lights dimmed. A coordinator tapped the mic.
"Welcome to Day Two of Reignite," the host boomed. "Let's talk emotional branding. And who better to show us than the people making us feel things in pixels?"
Sienna tuned out the intro. Olivia leaned in.
"How many times do you think he'll say synergy before someone throws a lanyard?"
"Three. Minimum. Five if there's a panel." Sienna muttered.

Then the case study reel began.

A montage. Split screens. Faces. Emotive campaigns. One photo lingered too long on the screen - a black-and-white image of a woman standing alone in front of a church. Wind blowing her coat sideways. Expression unreadable.

Her breath caught.

She knew that photo.

She'd seen it before, years ago. Online. In a gallery. Or maybe not.

Maybe it was in memory.

"Photo credit: Nico Morgan," the presenter announced.

Sienna froze.

Her stomach twisted. She turned slightly to Olivia.

"Did you see that name?"

"Nico, something? Yeah. Beautiful image. Why?"

"No reason," Sienna said, too quickly.

But her mind was already spiralling.

Nico. The same name. It couldn't be.

Olivia leaned over and whispered, "That the guy from the lounge?"

Sienna felt her stomach drop. "I never said."

"You didn't have to. You've got that face on. The one you get when you're connecting dots and trying not to look impressed."

Sienna shook her head. "It doesn't mean anything."

"Mmhmm," Olivia said, scrolling through her phone. "Well, if he's here and not speaking, I bet he's one of those hired creatives they slot into breakout rooms. Want me to stalk the programme?"

"No."

"Yes."

Sienna exhaled. "Fine. A little stalking."

"I found him. Listed under 'independent visual consultants.' Which sounds made up but expensive," Olivia said.

"Ok," Sienna replied.

"You ok?" Olivia asked.

"I don't know," Sienna admitted.

"Sexy name," Olivia added.

"That's unhelpful," Sienna said, deadpan.

"That's the brand," Olivia said with a shrug.

In the next breakout session, she saw him.

He wasn't on the screen or on the next slide; he was in person.

Across the room, leaning against a wall, like the whole thing bored him.

Dressed down again, dark jeans, navy shirt, that same stillness.

For a second, she watched him as if from outside herself.

The way his gaze scanned the room was slow, almost detached, until it landed on her.

A flicker of something passed between them. It was memory and chemistry, or the echo of one.

His head tilted slightly, like he wasn't surprised. Like this had always been part of the script.

He didn't wave or speak. He watched her the way he had the first night, like he already knew what she'd say next.

Her skin prickled beneath the fabric of her dress.

She turned away, suddenly too aware of herself. Of how easily he could see through whatever expression she'd managed to arrange.

But not before she saw the way his eyes lingered, not hungrily, or possessively, but like he was cataloguing her.

Like she was something he'd once had and wasn't quite sure how to hold again.

She walked briskly to the far side of the room and buried herself in the programme notes.

Words like "innovation tiers" and "brand architecture" meant nothing.

Not when her whole foundation felt like it had just shifted.

Because the photo was real.

Because something in her gut was lighting up like a flare.

Because she was starting to remember. And for the first time in a long time, she wasn't sure what scared her more: That she didn't know him at all.

Or that she already did.

TSR

Back in her room, she sat on the edge of the bed and pulled out her journal. She hadn't written in weeks. But now, her hand moved without asking.

He said his name like it wasn't mine, too.
The photo, I know it.

It wasn't merely familiarity; it was *recognition*. A gut-level memory, stubborn and unformed, hovering just beneath language. The kind of knowing that bypassed logic.

She didn't know what church it was, or what city. But she remembered the cold. The weight of the coat. The sound of wind against stone. And now, she wasn't sure how she knew that photo, where she had seen it… Or if she'd been the one standing in front of the lens.

There's something about the way he looks at me. Like he's waiting for me to catch up.

She closed the book before she could overthink it. She walked into the lounge. The door to Room 409 was shut. She pressed her palm to it for a second.

There was no sound or movement. But still, something that was not quite presence, and not quite memory. That pressure in the air when you stand near a turning point, and it hasn't turned yet.

She rested her forehead against the door, barely, letting herself hover in the in-between.

It would be easy to knock. To call out.

To follow the thread.

But easy wasn't always wise. And something in her, the part that still hadn't named what this was, knew:

If she stepped through too soon, the whole thing might vanish.

So, she stayed.

One more second.

Two.

Then she turned away.

She wasn't ready. But she was closer than yesterday.

Chapter Four

THE ALMOST MEMORY

That night, Sienna couldn't sleep properly. She hovered in that half-conscious state where thoughts dressed as dreams tried to make sense of themselves.

In one moment, Nico was in her hotel room, offering her wine with that maddening calm. In the next, he was behind a lens, pointing it at her, saying, "Hold still." And then she was running barefoot through cobbled streets, his name caught in her throat like a song she used to know. Somewhere European. Somewhere with history and heat.
She woke tangled in sheets, skin warm, breath short.
It was too early. But she got up anyway.

The air outside the suite had changed. It wasn't the temperature; it was something else. As if the hallway itself knew they'd reached a point of no return.
She dressed deliberately: black pants, black T-shirt, no jewellery. Her version of armour. At breakfast, she sat in the lounge alone, sipping coffee and pushing strawberries around a plate like they might confess something.
She heard the soft click of a door, Nico's. Then he stepped into the shared space, barefoot, holding two coffees again.
She didn't react. But she did clock the situation. He looked infuriatingly effortless. Like he'd just woken up in a cologne ad.

"Morning," Nico said, offering her coffee, like this was normal.

She took it. "You have a thing for silent entrances." She sipped the coffee. Black, strong and decent.

"And you have a thing for early starts."

Sienna gave him a look. "You realise you're fulfilling every cliché of the emotionally unavailable man, barefoot, mysterious, bearing caffeine."

He smiled. "You forgot charming."

"I never assume," she muttered, but her mouth twitched.

He sat casually. At ease, comfortable in a way that made her want to upend the table just to see if he'd react.

She took another sip. If nothing else, it was free coffee and better conversation than buzzwords and brittle egos.

"I saw your photo yesterday," she said.

He nodded, unsurprised. "I figured."

"You didn't say you were part of the conference."

"You didn't ask."

She narrowed her eyes slightly. "That's evasive."

He shrugged. "Maybe. Or maybe I wanted to see if you'd recognise it."

"I did."

A beat. Then she leaned in slightly.

"Have we met before?"

He didn't answer right away.

Instead, he said, "What makes you ask that?"

"The way you talk. The way you listen. The way you looked at me in the bar, like you were remembering something instead of seeing it for the first time."

Nico studied her face like he was matching it to a mental file.

"You really don't remember, do you?" he asked.

That made her pause, then her pulse kicked. "So, we have?"

He tilted his head. "Define 'met.'"

Sienna let out a short breath, half a laugh, half a threat.

"If we've met before, just say it."

He leaned forward, elbows on knees, coffee cradled in his hands.

"Have you ever been to Barcelona?"

She held her breath.

Once she had, years ago. A summer she didn't talk about. A time before everything became composed and calculated.

A boy.

A summer.

Her eyes flicked up to meet his. She looked at him, this time analysing. Then she saw him and for a second, time folded. The man in front of her wasn't a stranger; he was the echo of a summer she'd spent years pretending didn't matter.

Her breath caught, sharp and low. Her stomach dropped, in recognition, like her body had named him before her mind had. Fingers tingled. The air between them changed shape.

"I was twenty-two," she whispered.

He nodded.

The moment extended, neither one filling it. It was a full moment, full of things unsaid, things unremembered, things too sharp to be nostalgia all at once.

Sienna set her coffee down. "It was one summer."

Nico's voice barely carried. "One summer. That you ran from one morning."

She snapped to her feet. "I didn't run."

He didn't challenge it, which was worse.

"You knew who I was the moment you saw me," she said.

He unfolded himself from the chair. "I wasn't sure. Not until you opened the door."

"And you said nothing?"

"I wanted to see who you were now. Without the context. Without the memory."

She paced to the window, pulled back the curtain. The skyline of New York blurred slightly behind the glass.

"That summer," she said, not turning around, "feels like it belonged to someone else. A girl who thought a tan and a few witty lines were enough to keep the world at bay."

"She was brave," Nico said softly.

Sienna turned. "She was reckless."

He stepped closer. "She was real."

She hated how easily her throat tightened.

"This is wildly unfair. I don't have a line ready for this."

He smiled. "I'll take that as a compliment."

"There was a time I liked being reckless," she admitted. "Now I double-book my emotions with calendar invites and try to meditate them into submission."

He raised an eyebrow. "And how's that going?"

She exhaled sharply. "I'll let you know after my next existential spiral."

He didn't laugh; he watched her in that maddening way.

"I built an entire life pretending that time didn't mean anything," she said. "I assembled my own past like a press kit."

"And yet here we are," he said calmly.

She glanced at her now-lukewarm coffee. Her voice cracked, just enough for her to hate it; she'd been desperately trying to be witty and sarcastic to avoid this feeling that was rising inside her.

"Why now?"

"Because you're still her," he said.

He walked to his lounge door.

"I'm checking out today," he said.

That yanked something from her chest.

"Wait, what?"

"The hotel. I am checking out of the hotel, not the city."

She exhaled. "Where are you staying?"

He smiled. "If I tell you, you'll lose interest."

She stepped closer, something daring in her eyes. "Try me."

Nico paused at the door. "Come find me."

Then he was gone.

Sienna paced in her suite, the coffee cooling in her hand.

And this time, she didn't close the lounge door behind her.

She stared into the empty space between their rooms, then stepped forward and sat where he'd been.

The chair was still warm.

She glanced around the lounge, same marble table, same carafe of water half-full, same candle stubs from that first night, now unlit.

She imagined him walking through that door for the first time again.

Imagined what it must have felt like for him, seeing her, wondering if she'd recognise him, preparing for the moment she didn't.

She had her notebook. The leather-bound version she carried for moments like this, clarity. On the first blank page, she wrote:

Barcelona. 2000-and-something. Nico?

Then, almost impulsively, she scribbled beneath it:

I didn't forget. I stored it somewhere safer.

She tore out the page. Folded it. Slid it into the spine of his now-empty coffee cup.

It wasn't for him. But maybe one day.

Then she pressed her hand to the back of the chair for a second and finally closed the lounge door.

It didn't feel final, only like a pause.

TSR

Later that afternoon, Sienna sat in the hotel's library lounge, pretending to read a book she hadn't opened past the title page. The lobby buzzed faintly behind thick glass doors, a reminder that the city never stopped for anyone's emotional revelation.

Her phone vibrated. Olivia.

"*Are you alive or did that man in the shared lounge kidnap you?*"

Sienna smiled despite herself. "*Still in one piece. Emotionally porous, but upright,*" she replied.

"*Translation: you like him,*" Olivia wrote.

"*I don't know what I feel. I'm feeling it very loudly,*" Sienna replied.

"*Is this the part where I say, 'lean in' and 'don't overthink it' like a supportive woman from a Netflix show?*" Olivia teased.

"*Please don't. Just remind me that I'm not crazy,*" Sienna wrote.

"*You're not crazy. But you are underdressed for a romantic unravelling. Lipstick, please,*" Olivia replied.

"*Too late. I'm in noir mode,*" Sienna replied.

"*Christ. Someone stage an intervention,*" Olivia shot back.

"*You're useless,*" Sienna wrote, smirking.

"*Useless? Darling, I'm the Greek chorus to your slow-burn tragedy. Keep me posted*," Olivia replied.

Sienna laughed. She stared at the screen, thumb hovering like it was a trigger.

"I think I might've left something unfinished." Sienna typed.
"Him?" Olivia asked.
"Me," Sienna replied.

Then she sighed and dropped the phone into her lap. Across the room, a man in loafers was loudly ordering a turmeric latte with "vibe milk." She leaned back into the chair and let herself feel...
There were still panels to attend, people to impress, and strategies to articulate. But she no longer felt like producing, and that was something.

She pulled a magazine closer to pretend she wasn't re-evaluating every life decision since 2003. Maybe she didn't need a plan. Maybe she needed a stronger coffee and slightly worse instincts.

Across from her, a woman flipped through a design magazine, oblivious to the fact that Sienna's entire world had shifted a few feet to the left.
She closed the book. She already knew this chapter wasn't about fiction.
It was about memory.
And memory had just walked out of Room 409.

Chapter Five

FLASHBACK FRAME

Nico hadn't meant to stay this long in New York, not in that hotel, and certainly not in the space between two doors that felt too much like a memory dressed up in modern linen.

He told himself it was a coincidence. Told himself she wouldn't remember. Most people didn't. A summer, a name, a face, that was all it ever was to some. But not to him.

Barcelona. A heatwave. Cheap wine and cheaper cigarettes. Late nights that felt like lost pages from a book they'd both pretended not to have read.

She'd had a different rhythm then, or maybe a different laugh. Louder and less guarded. He'd watched her from across the courtyard of the hostel, the kind of place with flickering hallway lights and hand-scrawled Wi-Fi passwords. She'd been arguing with someone about the merits of Hemingway vs. Woolf.

He'd fallen a little bit in love right there, not because of her opinion (Woolf, passionately), but because she hadn't noticed him.
Until she had.

It was only a few weeks. Four, maybe. A shared breakfast, a beach trip, one night in a room with no air conditioning and a single fan that did nothing but whir a lullaby. They'd bought mangos from a market stall where the vendor refused to weigh anything properly, watched fireworks from a rooftop that wasn't theirs, and got lost looking for the cathedral, finding instead a courtyard of orange trees and stray cats.

One night, they walked back from the pier barefoot, shoes in hand, sharing a bottle of cheap rosé that tasted better than it should've. He'd read to her in Spanish, badly, and she'd laughed until her ribs hurt. And somehow, that small, imperfect stretch of time became everything she measured the rest against.

She'd kissed him like they had forever.
And left like they never existed.

He never got her last name. Just "Sienna." And even then, he wasn't sure if it was her real name or the one she wore that week.
But he kept the photo.

It wasn't staged; she didn't pose at all. She was leaning over a terrace balcony in the dying light, a glass of something in her hand, her hair pinned up haphazardly. She looked older than she was, perhaps timeless.
The image became part of a series that earned him his first feature.
"Women You Never Forget".
Of course, he didn't name her. He wouldn't.

But when she opened the door to Room 408, decades later, and looked at him like he was another stranger, he almost laughed.
The universe had a sick sense of humour.

He'd waited. Not to spring it on her. Not to say, "Remember me?" like some dramatic reveal.

He waited because he needed to see who she'd become. Whether she still had that laugh. Whether she still held her wine glass by the stem like it might tell her a secret.

And across two lounge chairs and a handful of almost-conversations, he'd seen her emerge.

The girl he remembered was still there.

Only now, she looked at the world like she'd stopped believing in magic but hadn't entirely given up on it.

She wasn't only older; she was sculpted by time. All the sharpness and softness working in tandem.

And he was different too.

Fifteen years in conflict zones, in famine belts, in places where hope was a luxury. He'd documented war, disaster, and grief. He remembered the pop of sniper fire in Damascus, the smoggy haze of bodies in Port-au-Prince, the heartbreak of mothers in Aleppo holding empty blankets.

Once, in South Sudan, he'd slept with one eye open for six weeks, waiting for aid that never came. In a burnt-out schoolhouse, a boy handed him a drawing of a tree that had no leaves. "It used to have fruit," the boy said. "Now it's waiting."

That photo never ran. It was too sad, too silent.

But he remembered. Because even when the world held its breath, something screamed.

After Yemen, he was done. The last job. A village razed by airstrikes. There were no survivors. Only a scarf in the rubble and the stench of grief.

He left his gear in the boot of a rusted-out Hilux and walked until his legs gave out. When he woke in a borrowed bed in Marrakesh, he emailed his editor one line: "No more people."

He stopped photographing faces and moved back to London. Then away again. He rented a cottage in the Cotswolds with ivy-covered windows and a peace that felt deserved.
He told himself it was peace.
Until her.

He hadn't planned on New York. It was meant to be a stopover; an art director friend had invited him to share a photograph at a conference he had declined last minute, but somehow still ended up flying out for. He told himself he wanted to visit galleries, see old colleagues. Maybe catch a train upstate and vanish for a bit. But really, he was drifting. London felt too sober now. His cottage had begun to feel like a waiting room for someone else's life. He'd spent months rearranging furniture and telling himself stillness was the goal. But that, without curiosity, was just another kind of noise.

He booked the hotel because it had a lounge and a reputation for discretion. That's what he thought he wanted.
Until she opened the door across from his.
Until he realised it wasn't boredom that brought him here.
It was unfinished business. He just hadn't known whose.
That morning, when she said, "Have we met before?" something inside him pressed pause.

Let her remember first, he thought, let her feel it, let it be hers, not his. Because the thing about memory is, it means more when you choose to keep it.

He sat now in his room, camera untouched, staring out at the skyline through the rain-speckled glass. He didn't know what came next. Whether she would run again. Whether she'd deny it all.
But he did know this:

Barcelona hadn't ended for him.

It had simply paused. And now, in this strange New York hotel, it was whirling again.

Like that fan in the old hostel, low, constant, and undeniable.

He remembered their last night in Barcelona. A thunderstorm had rolled in, roaring and theatrical, and they'd stayed up talking under a creaky ceiling fan, limbs tangled, hearts louder than the rain.

He told her about his camera; about the way light could soften a scar. She said nothing and traced his collarbone like she was trying to memorise it.

That final night in Barcelona had cracked something open in him. The fan barely worked. The heat was thick enough to taste. They'd pulled the mattress to the floor to be closer to the breeze, laughing as it thunked down beside their half-drunk bottle of wine.

She'd curled beside him with the unselfconscious ease of someone who'd claimed the space and him without asking permission.

He remembered her asking if he ever felt like he was meant for something bigger, then laughing like she didn't believe in anything at all. They hadn't talked about real life or real futures. They talked about light, music, and a poem she half-remembered.

He watched her fall asleep mid-sentence, her hand still resting on his collarbone. It wasn't sex that undid him; it was the harmony. The way she fit without effort. The sense that for once, nothing was missing.

When he woke, she was gone. She left before sunrise. A dent in the pillow.

All she left was the trace of possibility and a silence so loud it felt scripted. He never found out why she left. But in the years that followed, no one else ever quite managed to stay in the same part of his mind.

They existed, sure. But not in colour.

He had searched for a while. Called hostels. Asked around. But in a city built on secrets and shifting names, she became one more summer shadow.

And now, there she was. Across the lounge. Behind a door. In a hallway.
Still herself. Still unnamed in every way that mattered.
But he wasn't chasing this time.
He was waiting.
Because when she remembered, and he believed she would, it would no longer be a story she fled from.
It would be a story she finally chose to finish.
And this time, he would be there to help write the ending.

He took out the old photo again.
He never travelled with prints anymore. Everything lived in clouds and archives. But this one had stamped its permanence. The paper had faded at the edges; there was a faint crease across one corner from being folded and unfolded too many times. Still, she was there. Caught in amber light, alive in the frame. Her gaze wasn't toward the camera; it never was, but she looked like she was listening to something.
Sometimes he wondered what.
He'd never taken another photo quite like it.
Not even close.

He tucked it back into the notebook where he kept sketches, scraps, things he wasn't ready to lose.
Then he reached for his camera, just to hold it. He didn't want to shoot right away, but maybe soon.
She had remembered something. He could see it in her eyes.

The hesitation. The ache. The recognition just behind her sarcasm. And if she remembered one thing, one night, one moment, one heartbeat.

Then maybe she'd find the rest.

Chapter Six

NO MORE EDITS

The restaurant was mostly empty. The kind of place Olivia preferred: low lighting, strong drinks, and waitstaff who knew not to interrupt unless invited. Sienna swirled her wine and stared at the candle between them like it held a secret.

"You've been off," Olivia said. "Not just 'I hate my ex' off. Something else."

Sienna didn't look up. "You know how I feel about conferences."

"Right. And how you feel about hotel bars, shared lounges, and mysterious men with artfully rolled sleeves?"

Sienna's lips twitched. "You're reading too much into it."

"I'm reading just enough." Olivia leaned in. "Spill it. Start from the part where you know him."

Sienna exhaled. "I don't know him. Not... really. I just…" She stopped. Looked up. "Have you ever buried something so deep that you convinced yourself it was fiction?"

Olivia raised one brow. "You mean like my twenties?"

"I'm serious."

"So am I."

Sienna's voice dropped. "I think I knew him. Years ago. Barcelona. One of those summers that starts with 'it's just for fun' and ends with a flight you take too early without saying goodbye."

Olivia was silent. That rare, focused kind of silence she reserved for stories that mattered.

Sienna swirled her wine again. "I was twenty-something. Backpacking. Stayed in a hostel where the lights flickered, and the wine was cheaper than water. The air always smelled faintly of sea salt and cigarette ash, and the rooftop terrace had two broken chairs, one of which we claimed as ours. We'd sit under a sky the colour of wet slate, swapping stories about places we'd never been and futures we didn't yet know how to fear. He was there. We didn't even exchange full names."

"How romantic," Olivia said.

"How reckless."

"Same thing sometimes."

Sienna paused. Her eyes were glassy but dry. "I found out I was pregnant a few weeks later."

Olivia sat back, stunned.

"I didn't keep it. I didn't tell him. I didn't tell anyone."

Now Olivia sat back. "Not even your dad?"

Sienna shook her head. "He would've gone into lawyer mode. Solutions. Strategies. But no space for grief."

"And your mum?"

"She was gone by then."

"Oh."

"It was just me. In a walk-up apartment in Fitzrovia with too many stairs and too few blankets. I panicked. Made an appointment. Told myself it was a blip."

Olivia reached across the table. "You don't have to justify it."

"I know. But it's strange how one decision can shadow a whole decade, even if you never say it out loud."

They sat for a while. Two women in their forties, seasoned and sharp, but still carting around their younger selves like overstuffed handbags.
"Why now?" Olivia finally asked. "Why are you telling me now?"
Sienna looked over her shoulder, then back again. "Because I saw his name on the screen. And I recognised a photo; one he took in Barcelona. A moment I never thought I'd see again. It hit like lightning. The kind that doesn't ask permission before striking. I felt like someone had pulled a fire alarm in my chest."
"Jesus," Olivia replied.

"I've carried that version of me, twenty-two, scared, sunburnt, lying in a Barcelona hostel bed and tracing dreams on the ceiling. I buried her. Told myself she didn't matter anymore."
"You can tell her now. You still are her," Olivia said.

Sienna swallowed. The candlelight caught the edge of her glass, casting little golden ripples across the tablecloth.
"I always thought I had to be someone new to move forward," she said. "That being her meant being weak. Naïve. Reckless."
Olivia shook her head, gently. "Being her meant you felt everything. That's not weak. That's just human."
There was a long pause. Sienna looked past her friend, past the velvet-draped windows and into nothing.
"I thought if I never told anyone," she said, "then it wouldn't take up space in my life. But it did. It grew in the dark."
"And now?" Olivia asked.
"Now I think maybe... It's time to turn the light on."

The conversation between them was no longer weighted. It held space. Recognition. A strange sort of reverence.
"I'm glad it's you," Sienna said finally. "The one I told."
"Same," Olivia replied. "But let's be honest. I basically forced it out of

you with wine and guilt."

They both laughed deeply. Like women who knew what grief tasted like but also understood the relief of finally spitting it out.

Then the moment passed, not forgotten, but folded carefully into the night. Like something precious, no longer hidden.

"I remember walking away from the hostel," Sienna added suddenly. "I had one of those stupid paper maps. He was still asleep. I left a postcard; I didn't even write a note. I… left. I told myself it wasn't serious, so it wouldn't matter. But it did. For years, it did."

"Maybe it still does," Olivia said.

Sienna tilted her head. "Maybe."

She glanced at her phone.

"I think I need to go sit with this," she said.

"Sit with it. But don't stew in it," Olivia replied. "And for the record? You're still the bravest person I know."

Sienna didn't answer. But she smiled.

⚷
TSR

Back at the hotel, Sienna kicked off her shoes and flopped onto the bed, staring at the ceiling. Her mind was a cyclone, pulling fragments from that rooftop in Barcelona, the smell of smoke on linen, the salt-slick heat of skin she hadn't let herself remember in years.

Did she want to tell him? Did he deserve to know? Was there even a point, two decades and one forgotten summer later?

She opened her Notes app, typed three words:

He should know.

Then paused. Her finger hovered. The screen's glow caught her face, casting it in a strange kind of twilight.

She stared at the words as if they belonged to someone else.

Then she typed more:

He probably doesn't even remember.

Deleted it.

Typed again:

But I do.

Deleted that too.

She dropped the phone on the bed beside her and let out a slow breath.

What would she even say? "Hi, remember me? I disappeared after we slept together and then erased you from my history like a scandalous footnote. Surprise - I got pregnant."

She could almost hear Olivia snorting: Maybe don't open *with that.*

The truth was heavier now that it had been spoken aloud.

And Sienna wasn't sure if she wanted to carry it alone anymore.

Then typed again:

He probably does.

Then deleted that too.

She wasn't sure if she wanted closure or to keep circling the fire.

Olivia's voice replayed in her head: *"You can tell her now."*

Yeah, well, telling her was one thing.

Telling him? That was a whole other genre.

And yet… something in Sienna was shifting. The door she'd slammed shut was rattling in its frame.

She crossed to the mirror. Her reflection didn't look different, but something behind her eyes had tilted. She was no longer pretending she didn't remember Barcelona.

And maybe - just maybe - he wasn't pretending either.

She opened the lounge door. The air held, but not empty, like her past, waiting for her to walk in and finally stay long enough to name it.

The next morning, she woke early, showered, dressed, and left the hotel before she could talk herself out of it.

He'd said, *"Come find me."*

She didn't know what that meant. Nico hadn't left a clue or a note. He didn't leave a hotel name. He left that maddening, smirking instruction. It was the kind of thing men say when they already know you won't. But he didn't know her now. Didn't know how many layers she'd shed just to get back to the starting line.

Olivia had offered to come. Sienna said no.

She needed to do this alone.

She walked aimlessly at first, through SoHo, past cafes with chalkboard menus and tailored flower buckets. She checked a few boutique hotels, mostly out of instinct. Asked at a front desk or two. No luck. At one point, she spotted a gallery flyer bearing his name, but it was weeks old. Another dead end.

It was ridiculous, she knew. A city of over eight million people. She didn't have a plan or a map. She did have hope. Or something like it anyway.

By lunchtime, she was exhausted. She stopped in Bryant Park, sitting on the edge of a fountain, trying to pretend she'd just been out for a casual stroll, not an emotional scavenger hunt for a mirage in rolled-up sleeves.

Then she saw him.

Across the street.

Waiting.

Leaning against a lamp post like some tragic Parisian cliché, coffee in one hand, camera strap slung across his shoulder. He looked left. Looked right. Checked his phone. Looked up.

Saw her.

For one suspended moment, neither of them moved.

She half-raised her hand. Then dropped it. Panic bloomed behind her ribs.

She couldn't do this. Not now. Not like this.

She turned.

Walked quickly. Crossed at the lights. Didn't look back.

Behind her, Nico had already stepped forward.

But by the time he reached the corner, she was gone.

She reached the hotel lobby just before the afternoon lull. The air inside was cool, the kind of manufactured calm that tried to muffle everything real.

She moved past reception quickly, head down, unsure what she was even doing, until she heard a voice behind her.

"Excuse me," a man's voice said. "Did the woman in 408 leave already?"

Her spine straightened.

She didn't turn around. She kept walking toward the lifts, pulse tapping out a warning in her ears.

The receptionist replied, casual but firm, "She's still checked in. Would you like me to leave a message, sir?"

A pause.

Then Nico's voice again, low and certain.

"No."

He exhaled, slow and deliberate.

"Would you like to rebook, sir?"

He looked toward the elevator, then back at the desk.

"Yes," he said. "Same room. If it's still available."

Sienna stepped into the lift.

Let the doors close.

And for the second time in her life, she walked away from him without looking back.

Chapter Seven

THE LOUNGE DOOR CLOSES

She heard him return.

It did not originate from the hallway, but rather from a subtler source, a slight change in the atmosphere. The soft drag of luggage wheels across carpet. The faint click of a hotel room door.

Room 409.

He was back.

Sienna had one hand on the frame of the door to the lounge. She opened it, barely, a sliver of possibility. She could smell the faintest trace of his cologne, vanilla amber, familiar now in a way that made her feel ridiculous.

She didn't move further. She absorbed the scent, the sound, the echo of a presence she'd barely started to reckon with. Her fingers brushed the edge of the door, then curled inward like she was trying to hold something that no longer had shape. She let go.

Instead of crossing into the lounge, she grabbed the leather-bound notebook from the table and sat at the dining setting in her suite.

The door closed. Her pen hovered over the page but didn't move. She wasn't ready to write. She wanted answers, but on her terms. She wasn't going to be the girl who followed.

The air between the two rooms felt dense. Like the weather. Like pressure. She stared at the grain in the table, waiting, not for him, but for the version of herself that could handle this without falling apart. Then a knock. Soft. Three taps. The kind that could be mistaken for something else. She walked over and opened the lounge door just enough for her voice to pass through.

"What?"

He didn't speak at first. He waited.

She stepped back. Let the door open and walked in.

In the lounge, they sat across from each other. The space between them felt more strategic than easy, like a negotiation.

She didn't ask if he was the boy from Barcelona.

"You knew exactly who I was," she said. "From the second you saw me. Don't stand there like you didn't."

He looked down at his hands. He didn't deny it or make any confession of guilt.

"I wasn't ready," he said.

"Bullshit." Her voice cracked. "You let me spiral. You let me doubt myself. You stood there, cool as ever, while I felt like I was losing my mind."

"I didn't know how to bring it up."

"You didn't try. You watched me walk around this lounge like I was circling a memory."

"You were," he replied.

That cut more than she expected.

"I thought I was going crazy," she said. "I thought, maybe I was wrong. Maybe it wasn't you. Or maybe I wanted it to be. I don't even know."

"You knew," he said softly.

She swallowed. "Why didn't you say something?"

His voice dropped. "Because… maybe I wanted to see if you would finally choose me."

The words landed with a weight that knocked the air out of the room. She took a half-step back.

"That's not fair."

"No," he agreed. "It's not."

"I was a child."

"So was I."

"I didn't know how to stay."

"I didn't know how to ask you to."

Time stretched between them. It was raw, jagged.

"You're not him," she said. "He wouldn't have stayed silent."

He was weighted. He looked defeated, the weight of it all in his eyes.

"Maybe you're right," he said.

She bit her lip. Hard. That was the out, and he was giving it to her. She wasn't ready for that.

"You didn't even try," she said, voice small now.

"I waited," he said. "I watched. I hoped. But I didn't force it. Because maybe… I thought if you didn't remember, maybe it was better. Cleaner."

"It wasn't," she said.

He turned. For a moment, he seemed to gather himself, shoulders drawing in just slightly, as if bracing against something only he could feel. His gaze lingered on the floor, then the wall, anywhere but her. His hand hovered at the door, fingers tightening for a heartbeat before he let go. When he finally walked away, he was determined not to look back. No clever parting line, only space where he'd been, leaving only the echo of absence behind him.

She stayed seated for a moment. Breath held. Heart still pacing like it hadn't heard the gap settle.

Then, slowly, she stood.
Walked to the door.
And this time, she closed it.
She didn't slam it.
Closed.
Firmly. Finally.

And on the other side, in his suite, Nico sat very still.
Back to the door.
Eyes closed.
As if he'd just walked through a memory that chose not to hold him.

What neither of them saw, what neither of them could, was that they moved almost in sync. A mirrored retreat.

In her suite, Sienna sat with her back to the door, notebook in her lap, heart open and aching. On the other side, Nico mirrored her pose, spine pressed to his own closed door, knees bent, head bowed.

Two people. One room between them. So heavy it rang.
She almost reached out. Almost knocked. Almost opened the door again.
So did he.
But neither did.

They sat there. Back to back. Separated by a lounge of emotion and two decades of unspoken words.

And in that strange, breathless symmetry, they said everything.

After a long silence that felt like eternity, Sienna pushed herself upright, her legs stiff from sitting too long. She placed the notebook on the table, as if surrendering it, and walked to the bathroom to splash water on her face. The mirror gave nothing away. She didn't have red eyes or trembling lips. She was the same woman who'd walked into this hotel three days ago, except now every step forward felt like trespassing on a past she could no longer ignore.

She paced. Then stopped. Then paced again.
She even opened the minibar. Stared at the vodka miniatures. Closed it.
She returned to the table. Touched the notebook. Didn't open it.
Her fingers found her phone instead, flicking through apps like they might offer direction. But the screen reflected her face too clearly, and she hated what she saw. Not the lines or age or evidence of grief, but the hesitation. The unfinished things.

Sienna opened her messages, typed:
Are you awake?
Then deleted it.
Typed again:
I shouldn't have shut the door.
Deleted that too.
She placed the phone facedown. Walked to the window. Pressed her forehead against the glass.
She whispered aloud, to no one:
"I wanted you to knock again."

Across the lounge, Nico got up, stretched, and rubbed the back of his neck. His body ached in places it hadn't for years. He let out a breath, the kind you release when you're trying not to fall apart. Then he leaned his forehead against the door, closed his eyes, and he too whispered, but his words weren't meant for her; they were meant to fill the silence inside himself.

He slung the strap over his shoulder. Walked to the window on his side. The same view, the same fog. But different now.
He lifted the camera, pointed it vaguely out at the skyline, but didn't take a shot. He wasn't trying to capture anything. He wanted to feel something familiar in his hands. The weight. The stillness. The patience it had taught him.

He turned and scanned the room. His jacket was draped over the chair, the shirt she once touched still folded in his bag. Everything was ordinary, except for the way the air still felt like her.
Nico sat down again. Hands clasped.

"Say something," he murmured aloud. "Anything."
But there was only the noise of the air conditioning, and a door he wasn't ready to knock on again.

In her suite, Sienna sat on the floor, back to the wall. She picked up the notebook again and held it. She placed it over her heart like a shield.
Then lay back against the carpet, staring at the ceiling.
She mouthed the words she didn't say: *I looked for you.*
On the other side, Nico lay on the bed, staring at the same ceiling.
Two stories, one wound.

Neither of them slept.
When morning came, the doors stayed closed.
But the ache between them did not.

Chapter Eight

WHAT MIGHT HAVE BEEN

Silence. The kind that scratches at the inside of your skull and asks questions you can't answer.

Nico didn't knock again.

And Sienna didn't open the door.

For three days, they existed like shadows, next to, near, never with. The shared lounge remained untouched, the candles unlit, the carafe of water evaporating as if it too had grown tired of waiting.

Sienna filled her days with the mundane. Meetings, emails, and perfectly timed appearances at the conference. She overdelivered every conversation like her job was to prove she hadn't been gutted in a lounge chair three nights ago. Her fingers hovered over her phone too often. Her lip liner got more defined. Her heels got higher.

Olivia noticed, of course.

"You're spinning again," she said during one panel break. "Your energy is... Taylor Swift at the end of a tour."

Sienna arched a brow. "Is that a compliment or a medical concern?"

"A bit of both. You ok?"

"Peachy," Sienna said. "Just living my best emotionally compartmentalised life."

But the compartments weren't holding.

Back in her suite, she couldn't sit still. She reorganised her suitcase.

Deleted five email drafts to Nico she was never going to send. Tried to write in her notebook, but the words came out brittle.

On the third night, Olivia sent a single message:
"Lotus. Stillness. Don't burn down the hotel."
Sienna replied:
"Already lit the match."
Then: *"Still breathing. Still ridiculous."*
Then nothing.
Until the knock.
A knock at the main suite door.
Not the lounge, it wasn't Nico.
Three sharp raps, too confident to be room service.
Sienna opened the door.
Marc…Of course.

Tall, slick, and slightly too smooth, Marc wore his vanity like it belonged on a business card. Salt-and-pepper hair cut to red carpet spec. Jawline engineered for photo ops. He had the posture of someone who'd never been told no, and the wardrobe of someone who thought charm could be dry-cleaned back into rotation.
In a designer jacket, hands in pockets, wearing that expression that had once passed for charm. He didn't come with flowers and didn't carry a folder or an apology.
Typical.

She raised a brow. "What, did the concierge owe you a favour?"
He smiled. "Told them I was your husband."
"You were. Briefly. Like a migraine."
"I see you're still impossible."
"And I see you're still showing up where you're not wanted."
He took a step forward. "Can I come in?"

"No."

Another beat passed. He didn't move. He radiated entitlement.

"I heard you were in town," he said. "Thought we could talk."

"About what? How I've managed to stay successful without being orbit-adjacent to your ego?"

He gave a slow, measured smile. "You always did know how to rewrite history."

"No. I just stopped letting you write mine."

That wiped the grin off his face.

He glanced into the room, ignoring the hostility like it bored him. "It's a nice suite."

"It was. Then you arrived."

"I'm serious, Sienna. I have something real this time."

"Wow. Did you rehearse that?"

"I'm offering you a chance to come back, to build something with actual weight. Not just campaigns that disappear in a week."

"You think I'm here for relevance?"

"I think you're here alone," he said.

She paused. Did he really just say that?

And then, very calmly said, "You can leave now."

Marc held her gaze. For once, he had no comeback.

He turned, shrugged slightly like the conversation had been beneath him and walked away without looking back.

Sienna closed the door with finality.

She could have slammed the door, hoping it might have hit him somehow. Instead, she shut it. It wasn't worth her energy. She wasn't angry with Marc anymore or filled with heartbreak; just a clean line drawn in thick ink. Like closing a tab you'd forgotten was open.

She poured a glass of water instead of wine, although she could have had a *very* large glass, and took it out onto the balcony. The night air was cool but carried the weight of summer. Below, the city pulsed on without her.

She leaned on the railing, glass dangling from her fingers, and let the peace return, a steady peace, room to think.

Marc. Always so confident, that showing up was enough. Like, presence alone counted as accountability for him. He hadn't changed at all, which made things easier. The last time she'd let him back in, he'd promised transparency. Two months later, she found out he was rewriting pitches she'd already perfected, removing her name and inflating his own.

But that wasn't the beginning of the end. That was just the final proof.

They'd met at a launch party in Soho; he was magnetic, opinionated, and already on every media list that mattered. She was hungry, newly promoted and still wearing heels that blistered by noon. He called her brilliant in front of a Vogue editor. She mistook that for respect.

The marriage was a highlight reel, forged and clean. Magazine spreads painted them as the next creative power couple, dynamic, disruptive, and desirable. There were photo shoots on yachts they couldn't afford, quotes they never said, and a signature cocktail named after them at some launch they didn't stay for. Their wedding hashtag trended for eight hours.

But behind the scenes, she was shrinking. Marc treated her ambition like a phase and her ideas like rough drafts. He took credit with a smile and shared blame. When she got awards, he said the whole team should be recognised. When he got them, he framed every plaque.

And still, she'd tried. Therapy, time apart, gentle redirection. Nothing shifted. Because Marc wasn't interested in evolving, he was interested in staying adored.

They'd married fast. Too fast. A press whirlwind, joint interviews, and magazine spreads that told a story far cleaner than the reality. In private, he was impatient. Dismissive. The kind of man who said "don't overthink it" every time she asked a question he didn't like. Their fights weren't explosive; they were clinical. Controlled. But they chipped away at her.

He cheated. She was a junior creative who was barely out of college, and who thought Marc's charm was substance. Sienna hadn't even confronted him. She didn't need to. The timeline told her everything. The meetings that ran late, the vague travel. The sudden interest in cologne again.

The last straw wasn't even the betrayal at work. It was the night he laughed, actually laughed when she told him she wanted to start something on her own.

"Sure," he'd said, smiling like it was sweet. "Just don't expect me to fund your little detour."

She had walked out that night. Took her laptop, her charger, and a face mask. Slept on Olivia's couch for two weeks while she mapped her future out on the back of takeaway menus.

He'd never said sorry. Only "you're being dramatic."

And now, he was back. With nothing but recycled charm and a half-formed pitch.

TSR

The next morning, she sat by the window in the hotel café with a black coffee she didn't finish and a news app she didn't want to open. Her name was mentioned in two articles, both about the campaign, both quoting her old job title like it still defined her.

She bookmarked neither.

Instead, she scrolled through her own camera roll. Photos of mock-ups, mood boards, scribbled ideas on napkins. An archive of proof: she'd done this herself. Without him. Without anyone.

And yet. The photo that caught her eye wasn't from a campaign. It was of her. Hair in a messy bun. Eyes wide and laughing. Olivia had taken it at some rooftop thing months ago. Sienna couldn't even remember what was so funny.
But she remembered that version of herself. Unfazed and present.
Then her phone buzzed.

Olivia (voice note): "Ok, full pep talk incoming. You are not just the main character. You're running the whole show. That man is a paperclip, Sienna. A bent one. I love you. That's all."

Sienna smiled. She texted back: *Is it weird that I don't even feel angry? I feel… clean.*
Olivia replied. *"That's growth, babe. Also, I'm still egging his car. Emotionally."*

She went back upstairs. She reached for her notebook, flipped it open to a blank page. The pen hovered.
She wanted to write something to Nico:

Some men only come knocking when you've already rebuilt the house. Doesn't mean they get a key.
Then:
You were a maybe. He was a loud mistake. I see that now.
Her hand paused. The pen tip tapped once against the paper.
And then she wrote one more line:

If you still see me, Nico, I hope it's the version that walked away.
She let the pen fall into the crease. Closed the notebook gently and walked to the lounge door.
Still closed.
She didn't open it. But this time, she didn't look away either.
She leaned against the frame, eyes steady.

This didn't scare her tonight. She was still here. Still her.

She reached out. Turned off the hallway light.

And walked to bed in the dark, unafraid, undiminished.

Chapter Nine

THE PITCH

Sienna wasn't sure why she said yes to dinner.

It wasn't forgiveness, and it sure as hell wasn't interest.

Marc had called her suite the next morning, somehow still confident, still smooth. *"Let me try again,"* he'd said. *"Just one dinner. Off the record."*

She should've hung up. Instead, she'd said, *"One hour. One drink."*

It wasn't that she was tempted. She wanted to see what angle he was playing. Because part of her wanted to watch him try and fail.

She dressed in the same black dress from the campaign afterparty. She wasn't trying to make a statement; she wanted to look like a *weapon* in it. Red lipstick. Hair slicked back. She checked her reflection once, then turned away before she could second-guess the decision. Her phone buzzed.

It was Olivia. *"Just remember who you are and who he still isn't."*

"Relax. I'm not going for romance. I'm going for data," Sienna replied.

"Surveillance mission. Got it. Will be on standby with an emotional extraction plan," Olivia said.

O━┱
TSR

The restaurant was dim and sleek. That modern kind of chic where the napkins had folds so sharp they looked like origami, and the wine list came on a tablet. Sienna arrived three minutes late. Deliberately. Marc was already at the table, standing when he saw her, jacket draped over the chair beside him.

"You look incredible," he said.

She slid into her seat. "I always do."

He chuckled and motioned to the waiter. Without consulting her, he ordered their drinks: pinot for her, Scotch for him, and some absurdly overpriced appetiser involving truffle foam.

"You still love that wine," he said.

"Do I?" she replied, arching a brow.

There was a lull.

The waiter returned. The wine was wrong. She didn't say anything. Instead, she looked around. A couple two tables over were arguing, but softly so no one could hear. A man with a laptop was talking to himself between mouthfuls of pasta. Across the room, a familiar face, one of the campaign photographers, gave her a subtle wave. She nodded back. Marc launched into small talk. Sydney, acquisitions, who had lost which account. He was charming in that manicured way, like he'd spent too long watching himself speak. She let him talk. Sipped her not-quite-right wine. Reapplied her lipstick in the reflection of a butter knife. A hotel staff member tripped and broke the tedious moment of waiting for what Marc was going to spin. A tray of cutlery clattered across the marble floor like a cymbal crash at the end of an awkward joke. Everyone turned. Marc flinched. Sienna didn't.

"You've changed," he said.

She looked at him. "No. I've stopped apologising."

The appetiser arrived. She didn't touch it. Instead, she asked, "What's the pitch?"

He smiled. He was ready and eager.

"It's bold," he said. "Retail, tech, fashion; merging them in a way no one's done before. Pop-up integration, sustainability built in, a data loop feeding instant consumer feedback. Physical-to-digital immersion. And it needs a face people trust. Someone with your edge. Someone who knows how to spark cultural relevance and land the message where it matters."

She leaned back. "So, this dinner is a job interview with breadsticks."

Marc hesitated. "It's a chance to start again. A chance to make something meaningful. I've got a few big names circling, one in Berlin, two out of New York. Funding isn't the issue. The issue is tone. The issue is leadership. That's where you come in. You've always been the differentiator."

She tilted her head. "You mean I made you look credible."

He didn't deny it.

"I'm not asking you to come back to what we were," he said. "This is new. Separate. Equal. I've got three concepts drafted, two brand collaborations lined up, and the tech guys are already building the prototype. I want you as Creative Director. Co-founder. Your name first this time."

He leaned in. "We'll start small, exclusive launches, established markets. Think curated AI fashion matches to physical pieces in real time. Facial data as a customer journey entry. Real-time heat maps of trend responses. And you, your aesthetic, your brand power leading that story."

He kept talking. UX funnels. Interactive mirror tech. Loyalty encoded on blockchain. On paper, it was ambitious. Smart, even. But she knew Marc. And she knew desperation when it smiled this wide.

Sienna let him talk while she ran her fingers along the stem of the wine glass. This was all a charade. He didn't want her input; he wanted her presence.

She cut in, "Is there a board already?"

Marc paused. "Preliminary. Nothing locked in."

"And how long have you been using my name to sell this fantasy?"

He laughed a little too quickly. "It's not a fantasy. It's an inevitability. With you, we fast-track the whole structure. With you, I get instant credibility."

"You mean I get to do the work while you collect the applause?"

"You know I respect your work," he said.

"You *used* my name, Marc. You didn't ask. You decided."

He slid a folder across the table, glossy mock-ups, flow charts, decks she'd seen a thousand times in a thousand failed ventures. Except this one had her name on the first page. Her photo on the second. Marc had already used her image to pitch.

She picked up the folder and flipped through it. On one page, a mission statement with language she would never use. On another, a product rendering that looked suspiciously like a recycled concept from a startup she'd advised two years ago.

"You've been shopping this around," she said.

He hesitated.

Sienna didn't speak again straight away. Her thumb rested against the edge of the folder, but her gaze had shifted somewhere else entirely. She was back in their old office, the open-plan fantasy Marc had sold to investors. She remembered the way he'd introduce her to clients as "the magic behind the curtain" but never let her speak first in a pitch.

The time he rewrote her copy for a campaign and sent it out under his name. The moment she knew she had to leave was solid. A Tuesday. She'd just spent seven hours crafting a deck for a client she'd fought hard to secure, only for Marc to say, "It's good, but I think it sounds too... feminine."

Now, watching him sit there, still confident, sleek, it struck her: he hadn't changed because he'd never had to. The world had always handed him second chances wrapped in silk. And she had once handed him hers.

She closed the folder. "You included my name without asking."

"You don't want a partner, Marc. You want a human shield with industry clout."

He frowned, confused. "That's not fair."

"No," she said. "But it's accurate."

Marc exhaled, half-smiling. "It gave us traction. You're still gold in this market. Don't be naïve, this is how it works."

"Wrong," she said. "That's how *you* work."

She studied him. He looked proud. Like he'd just offered her the world, and all she had to do was step back into orbit.

"I've missed this," he added.

"You missed relevance," she replied. "Let's not confuse the two."

He blinked.

"You didn't love me, Marc. You loved what I made you look like."

Sienna straightened, drawing herself up to her full, formidable height.. But then she paused.

From the corner of her eye, she saw movement near the back of the restaurant. Through the glass panels that divided the dining room from the hotel piano bar, someone was playing. Low, melodic. Minor key. A familiar shape.

Nico.

He hadn't noticed her yet. He was seated, back straight, fingers moving with precision. Playing something, Sienna couldn't place, but it felt like a memory.

Marc followed her gaze.

"What's that?" he asked.

She didn't answer. Her hand hovered over the back of her chair. Then she stepped away.

"I'm done here," she said.

"Sienna," he said.

"Dinner's on you," she said. "So was the damage."

She walked toward the music.

Behind her, Marc watched her go but didn't follow. He looked between her and the man at the piano. Something shifted in his expression. Not quite realisation. But close enough.

And then it hit him.

He didn't say it aloud. But it settled in the tightness around his jaw, the way his shoulders pulled back, defensive. Marc wasn't used to being the one left behind. The idea didn't fit him. He had always assumed he was the ending. The full stop and not the footnote.

What he felt wasn't heartbreak. Narcissists don't break. What he felt was insult. A wounded ego. Confusion wrapped in disbelief. That she had not only moved on but moved *up*. Without him.

It wasn't the rejection that stung. It was the fact that she meant it. That she had no intention of circling back.

He remained there for a beat too long, watching her disappear into something unscripted.

Sienna entered the piano bar, shoulders squared.

Chapter Ten

JUST ONE SONG

The piano bar had a hush to it, unlike the fake kind you find in luxury lounges; this was real, heavy and reverent. The sort that settles over people when they realise something rare is unfolding.

Sienna stepped inside, heels barely audible against the black tile. The room was candlelit and low-ceilinged; the bar itself was lined with cut-glass bottles that threw prisms across the back wall. And there, at the grand piano in the far corner, was Nico.

He hadn't seen her yet.

He was playing something stripped, low and aching.

"Calling You" from *Bagdad Café*, that haunting, yearning stretch of melody. No lyrics, only notes and breath and everything unsaid. It shouldn't have fit here, among the corporate men with whisky tumblers and couples trying not to fight. But it *did*. It wrapped around her, slowed her heartbeat, and made the room feel like it was underwater.

Sienna watched him. She didn't know he played. She should have. It was exactly like him, understated, exacting, and brilliant.

His hands moved like they remembered things his body was still deciding whether to feel. Eyes closed, head tilted slightly, composed but vulnerable. He looked nothing like the twenty-two year old she ran from. And yet, exactly like him.

When the last note landed, he opened his eyes. And saw her. The space between them folded in on itself, like a held breath waiting for release.

"Just one song," he said.

She stepped forward.

"That's all it ever took."

Nico pushed back from the keys as she approached; there was neither a kiss on the cheek nor an obligatory embrace. But a stillness that felt more honest than anything they'd shared in years. He pulled out the bench again for her, and she sat. He stayed standing a beat longer, hands in his pockets, the posture of someone who didn't know if he had permission to unfold.

"I wasn't sure you'd come," he said, voice low, unforced.

"I wasn't sure you'd still be here," she replied.

"I wasn't," he admitted. "But I came back."

She looked up. "Why?"

He glanced at the piano. "Because I thought if I played the right thing, you'd hear it."

"You were always better at saying things without words."

"That used to be enough," he said. "Back then."

She looked at him for a long moment. "You remember it all, don't you?"

"Barcelona. The hostel. The broken fan. The mirror that made us look taller. The storm that took the power out for six hours," he said.

Sienna let out a breath. "I kept the postcard."

"The church steps," he said softly. "I wrote two words."

"Still here."

"But you weren't," she said.

"I thought you made a choice," he said. "I thought you didn't want to be found."

"I thought you stopped looking."

He sat beside her. Closer than before, not touching.

"I didn't know how to ask you to stay," he said.

"I didn't know how to stay without losing myself," she said.

"That's the cruel part," Nico said, turning toward her. "You left before you could love me."

Sienna stared. "No. I loved you before I knew what that meant."

It was the sound of two people re-entering the same story.

What happened after Barcelona didn't break all at once. It came undone, thread by thread.

"I waited," Nico said. "At the hostel. For two days."

Sienna's eyes didn't move. "I know."

"I told myself you'd lost your phone. That you'd reach out eventually. That you hadn't really left, that you'd change your mind."

"I did change my mind," she said. "Twice. Once on the platform, and again at the airport."

"So why didn't you come back?"

"Because I didn't want to be the girl who came back."

Nico nodded, like he was translating her answer into a language he finally understood. "You were always more fearless than me."

She turned to him. "No, I was just better at pretending."

He didn't ask about the years in between, and she didn't offer. That was the thing about absence: it fills in its own gaps. You imagine versions of each other that never age, never disappoint.

But now they were sitting here. Older. Sharper. He looked like a man who had lived several lives since, and she felt like a woman who had survived hers.

"I should've found you," he said.

"I should've stayed," she replied.

They sat with that, to honour the truth of it.

"We turned each other into unfinished stories." He said.

"Worse," she said. "We made assumptions."

The piano between them felt too small now for the weight of what remained.

And yet, neither filled the space with excuses. Because maybe the hardest part wasn't leaving.

Maybe it was what they'd done after, had they finally said enough.

It wasn't the reunion either of them had imagined, not that they would admit to imagining it at all.

There were no sweeping declarations or apologies served with candlelight. She was a woman who once ran, and he was a man who once let her. Sitting side by side like the ending had never finished writing itself.

It was raw.

It wasn't about anger or blame, more like the ache of old bruises you didn't realise were still healing.

The kind of pain you only feel when you realise you've numbed it too well for too long.

Nico's hands rested on his knees, fingers tapping an invisible rhythm, the same way they had on her thigh that night they sat on a Barcelona rooftop with wine they couldn't afford.

The memory was so sharp she winced.

He noticed.

"Do you remember that rooftop?" he asked.

"Where we made a list of things we'd do differently?"

"And then did none of them," he said.

Sienna gave a soft laugh. "Except the part where we promised to be honest."

"We weren't."

"Not even a little."

That was the nostalgia of it, how young they were in their certainty. How fragile they'd been. How intimate the unravelling had felt, even when it was breaking them.

And yet, it was bittersweet.

Because they were here now, wiser and wearier, knowing they had survived everything except each other.

"We weren't ready," she said, almost to herself.

"But it still mattered," he said.

She looked at him, finally letting herself. His eyes had the same weight, the same impossible steadiness. But now she could meet them without looking away.

There was no fixing what had been lost. But there was something in the ache that felt necessary.

As if the pain had been part of the point.

Sienna stood up, and it shifted the moment. Nico looked up, unsure if she was leaving again.

She wasn't.

"Come on," she said, voice steady. "Walk with me."

He followed without a word, the piano bar dissolving behind them as they crossed the lobby. The air was different now; suspended, as if the hotel itself knew not to interrupt.

They entered the lift together without speaking. It was late now, close to midnight, and the hotel had gone still. There was no more event chatter or lobby music; there was the hush that happens when the city is finally too tired to impress anyone.

Sienna hit the button for the floor. Nico said nothing. The doors closed.

The soft ding of each passing floor felt ritualistic. For a moment, it was just the soft mechanical whir, the mirrored walls, and the breath between them. She felt it before she saw it, how close he was standing. It felt like he was not doing it deliberately; it was natural. Like he still remembered how she used to lean back against him when lifts made her nervous. Like his body hadn't forgotten her after all.

She turned her head slightly. His eyes were already on her.

"You always did prefer silence to small talk," he said.

"Only when it's with someone who deserves the quiet."

He smiled, a new smile which was smaller, it felt sadder and more honest.

The lift shuddered briefly as it reached a floor, then stopped. It did not stop on their floor, it just… stopped.

The lights dimmed. A pause.

"Seriously?" she muttered, pressing the button again.

Nothing.

She looked at him. "Did you plan this?"

"If I had, there'd be champagne."

Sienna laughed. It bounced off the walls and surprised them both.

"We're stuck," she said.

"We've been stuck for years," he replied.

That pulled her eyes back to his. The moment turned.

"I hated you," she whispered.

"I know."

"I hated myself more."

"I didn't."

He reached for her hand to touch the edge of it with his fingers, feather light.

She didn't pull away.

The air changed again. Tension, heat, history, all of it pooled in that tiny space like it had been waiting to be noticed.

When the lift jolted back to life, they didn't move apart.

As the doors reopened, Sienna breathed in deeply, so deep it was grounding.

"Let's go."

And this time, she meant forward.

They stepped out of the lift as if emerging from a dream, charged and changed. The hallway was empty. Soft lights stretched shadows along the carpet, and the sounds of the building returned like background music, cueing the next scene.

Her room, his room, the lounge, the one between their rooms. The place that had become a no-man's land.

"I'm not inviting you in," she said, over her shoulder.

He didn't take offence. "I wouldn't expect you to."

She turned into the lounge.

It was empty, lit only by the soft lamps they'd once left flickering. The carafe of water still sat on the sideboard, full. She poured a glass and handed it to him without asking.

He accepted it. "Is this the part where we pretend we're just neighbours again?"

"No. This is the part where we stop pretending anything."

He moved closer; his intention was to stand near enough to be felt. The air between them thickened.

"I kept wondering," she said, "if I made it all up. If you were just a version I built in my head because I wanted the story to mean something."

"It meant something," he said.

She looked at him, daring herself to believe it.

Nico held her gaze. "Tell me the truth now."

Her throat tightened. "I will. But not here."

And for the first time, this felt like an invitation and not exile.

Sienna led, barefoot now. She'd slipped her heels off at the piano, and somehow, they'd never returned. Nico followed at a respectful distance, far enough to let her decide how this played out.

At the suite door, she stopped.

Her hand rested on the handle, and she looked back at him.

"This is the part where you ask me what comes next," she said.

He didn't. He waited.

She opened the door but didn't step inside.

"Give me five minutes," she said. "I'll knock."

A pause. Then she added, "Next door. Not the lounge."

He nodded once. He didn't push back or make any assumptions.

She stepped in, closed the door behind her, and leaned against it, head

tilted back, eyes closed. Everything in her throbbed, her temples, her
throat, the place in her chest that still remembered him like a song.
She poured herself a glass of water and walked toward the window. The
city still shimmered beneath them, unaware of the turning tides in one
small hallway above it.
She needed to breathe. Needed to remember who she was and what
she wasn't willing to give away because history knocked.
But also, this was different now. She was different now.
And he had waited.

She walked to the mirror. Smoothed her dress. Wiped away the smudge
of mascara under one eye. In the glass was a woman deciding, fully
awake.
She opened her notebook.
One line only:
I think I'm ready to tell you now.
She closed it.
And knocked, three soft taps, this time on his door.
She didn't go halfway. This was not going to be maybe. She waited.
And from the other side, the handle turned.

Chapter Eleven

THE TRUTH BETWEEN ROOMS

The door closed behind them with a soft click, but it felt louder than it was.

Sienna stepped into the room. Nico hovered at the entrance like he wasn't sure if he should let her all the way in.

She didn't wait for an invitation. She moved past the table by the window and stopped in the centre of the room. The lamp beside the bed cast a warm, quiet light. Everything else waited. Even the air.

He watched her like she might vanish again.

"I didn't come here for sympathy," she said, not facing him.

"I didn't assume you did," he replied.

Sienna exhaled, as if the air had to be measured to survive what came next.

"I didn't just leave Barcelona," she said. "I left *you.*"

Whatever it broke in him, he didn't show it. She turned finally; her arms folded. "And I did it, without warning, just one line on a postcard I didn't think you'd keep. I disappeared; I had to go."

Nico's jaw shifted. He was, remembering. Folding on the inside. But being here was too important, and the waiting was the only thing keeping him upright.

"I was twenty-two," she said. "Stupid, scared, and suddenly pregnant."

Nico was anchored and infinite, broken and alive all at the same time.

"I found out a few weeks after I got back. My whole life was still in pieces, and the only thing I was sure of was that I wasn't ready to be anyone's mother. Especially not with you on the other side of the world and me too cowardly to pick up the phone."

She looked away.

"It wasn't about shame. Or hiding. I just... couldn't carry it. The pregnancy. The weight of it. I didn't see a world where that child would've had anything close to what they deserved."

Now her voice wavered.

"And I've thought about them. Not every day, but often enough to know that I can't pretend it didn't happen. I didn't regret the choice. But I mourned the version of myself that made it."

"I didn't just leave because I was scared," she said. "I left because I couldn't watch your face change when you realised I wasn't ready, and you were."

Her voice didn't break. It didn't need to. The weight was in the words themselves.

Nico said s nothing, giving her space. That was always his gift.

"I was barely out of college," she continued. "I came home confused, certain only that part of me hadn't made the flight back."

Her tone had that sharp clarity, the kind that comes only when you've said something a thousand times in your head and never out loud.

"A few weeks later, I took the test," she said. "I didn't tell anyone. Not even Olivia. I just stared at the stick like it was someone else's future."

"I sat with it. For hours. Days. I imagined telling you, over the phone or in some ridiculous email you'd have to translate twice to understand what I meant." She almost smiled. "I tried to write it. I really did."

She looked at him then.

"I didn't want to be someone's mistake," she said. "I didn't want you to panic or feel trapped or fly across the world out of obligation. And I sure as hell didn't want to be the reason you stopped being you."

She let it settle before continuing.

"I made a decision. And I made it alone. Because I couldn't picture bringing a child into the world with that much fear already built into it.

Not with everything half-written. Not with love I hadn't named yet."

Sienna stepped toward the table, brushing the edge with her fingers, ready to hold on tight in case she fell.

"I'm sorry for not telling you," she said, "that part's mine and I carry it forever."

Nico's hands were at his sides, fists barely clenched. He felt helpless. He opened his mouth, then closed it.

Then finally:

"I would've come."

Three words. Steady. Devastating and true.

"I didn't leave because I didn't care," Sienna said. "I left because I wasn't ready to stay."

Nico didn't speak, and he couldn't move. But something behind his eyes shifted, recognition, maybe. Or something older. Something he'd been carrying without a name.

"It wasn't just fear," she said. "It was protection. From you. From me. From the version of my life that suddenly felt like it was veering off course and I wasn't driving anymore."

She crossed the room; she needed to move because staying still made it harder.

"I told myself that if I told you, it would ruin you. That you'd drop everything, chase me, propose, try to fix it. And I knew part of me would let you. I was terrified of that."

She turned back to face him. Her arms were folded; she was trying to keep the shape of herself intact.

"I didn't trust myself to stay me if I stayed with you."

Her words weren't meant to hurt. They were facts she'd lived with for too long.

"I couldn't give you the chance to say the wrong thing. Or the right one. Because either way, I'd have stayed. I would've folded my life into yours and called it love."

She shook her head. "I was still trying to find my shape. If I stayed, I would've become someone's girlfriend, someone's mother, someone's problem. I didn't want to be a cautionary tale. I wanted to become someone I could live with."

Nico exhaled, but still said nothing.

"And maybe that was selfish. But I needed to survive me first."

Nico sat down, like his body needed anchoring. His elbows braced on his knees, hands interlaced, not from fury, but from something deeper. He didn't raise his voice. But the stillness in him crackled.

"I knew something was wrong that morning," he said. "I went to get coffee. You were still sleeping, hair in your face. I remember thinking I'd bring back those pastries you liked, the ones you pretended not to eat. But when I came back, you were gone."

He looked up at her then. "No note, none of your belongings, just the absence of you."

"I checked the hostel. The corner store. The markets. I asked three shopkeepers if they'd seen you. One of them said maybe, another shrugged. I ran to the church. You weren't there. I waited two hours. Told myself you would come back."

He gave a dry laugh. "Then I stopped making excuses."

His hands moved now, restless, tracing shapes in the air. "I went to the train station, remember? That dusty old one. I described you to the woman at the ticket desk. Blonde, sharp tongue, walks like she owns the pavement. She asked if you were my girlfriend. I said, 'I don't know. I hope so.'"

He exhaled. "I asked the hostel. They said you checked out early. Left a key and a postcard. I thought - ok. Ok, she's running. But maybe she wants to be found."

He pulled something from his wallet, thin with age. Unfolded it gently. Sienna's throat closed.

It was the postcard. The one she thought she'd tossed.

"Thanks for the summer," he read aloud. "No name. No return address."

His voice cracked. "I spent a week walking Barcelona. I wasn't sightseeing. I was just... looking. Bus stations, cafés, hostels. Anywhere with a door you might've passed through. I went to the airport twice. Stood there like a fool, scanning faces. Hoping."

Sienna's heart thudded in her chest.

"I wasn't angry," he said, softer now. "I was scared I'd imagined it all. That you were some brilliant glitch in my life. A dream."

He looked at her; he didn't feel resentment, but he felt something far harder to bear.

"You weren't a fling to me, Sienna. You were the thing that made sense. And you disappeared."

The swell of heartache rising from within their bones made the air feel as if the world had just exploded into millions of pieces, and the distance between them wasn't measured in inches; it was years, absences, possibilities never spoken aloud.

"When I came back, and you were gone," he said, "I thought it was something I said. Something I did. I spent hours replaying our last night like it was a scene I'd missed something in."

Sienna didn't interrupt.

"I walked every part of that city for days. I had nothing but a first name and a memory."

He laughed, but there was no humour in it.

"I didn't even know how to be angry. I just felt hollow. Like whatever version of myself I was with you - he'd been erased overnight."

Sienna's throat tightened. She looked at the floor.

"I wasn't ready," she said.

"I know," he replied.

Then, softer: "But I was."

He sat down, as if the weight of everything he hadn't said in two decades had finally caught up to him.

"You weren't just a fling, Sienna. You weren't something I was going to forget after a few drinks and a new city. You were... vivid. The kind of person who leaves fingerprints on your life, even when they're gone."

She looked at him, really looked. "You make it sound like I was perfect."

"You weren't," he said. "You were real. And that was enough."

She crossed the room, then stopped short. "And now?"

He didn't answer right away.

"I still see her," he said. "The girl on the rooftop in that ridiculous orange skirt. The one who laughed too loudly and told me I was full of shit when I called her beautiful."

Sienna smiled. "That skirt was iconic."

He smiled. "It was. So were you."

And in that moment, there were no confessions or declarations. There was an understanding. That what they had mattered. That it left something behind in both of them.

That maybe, just maybe, it wasn't done yet.

That rare, sacred hush settled between them again; when two people realise the air they're breathing is different now.

Sienna stood near the small table by the window, eyes unfocused. Nico remained seated on the edge of the bed, elbows on his knees, hands clasped. Neither moved to fill the space. It didn't need fixing.

"I used to wonder what I'd say if I saw you again," he said, finally. "But none of the things I practised made it past the door."

She glanced sideways. "That's probably for the best."

He smiled, then sobered. "You know what's strange? For years, I thought I imagined you. That I'd romanticised a summer. Made too much of a brief thing."

He paused, "I realise now I made too little of it."
She sat down across from him, legs crossed, one arm draped casually over the back of the chair. But her eyes, her eyes weren't casual at all.

"I don't want you to feel sorry," she said. "For what I did. Or didn't do."
"I don't," he said. "I feel... like we've both carried different versions of the same memory."
Sienna's gaze dropped to her hands. "It's hard to explain to someone what it's like to choose yourself and still grieve what might've been."
"That explains everything," Nico said.

The room sat with the kind of truth that doesn't demand resolution. Just two people sitting in the stillness, acknowledging the gravity of what they'd shared; and lost; and survived anyway.
"I don't know what this is," she whispered.
"You don't have to," he said. "We're not the people we were."
"No," she agreed. "But I'm not scared of the room anymore."
He nodded. He walked toward the small minibar, pulling out two tiny bottles of whisky and soda, poured them into glasses and handed her one without a word.
"To honesty," he said.
She clinked her glass gently against his. "To finally speaking."
They drank. It wasn't good. But it didn't need to be. The truth, for the first time in years, was enough.
Nico set his glass down. His fingers lingered on it, tracing the rim, a habit she recognised. He used to do that with wine glasses in Barcelona, circling them like he was trying to summon clarity.

Sienna walked toward the door. She wasn't leaving, she was moving. Trying to stretch out a moment that had somehow become heavier than it was before.

She turned back to him. "Do you ever wonder? What it would've looked like…if I'd stayed."

He looked up. "Every version." He hesitated, then: "I used to imagine it was perfect. Then I hated myself for doing that. For pretending life ever is."

Her throat tightened. "It wouldn't have been."

"I know."

She stepped closer. Sat down beside him this time. Their shoulders didn't touch, but the distance was gone.

"I'm not sorry I didn't come back," she said.

"I'm not sorry I waited," he said.

The space between their hands felt different, something that was intentional, conscious and soft.

"I'm still figuring things out," she said, voice lower now. "That hasn't changed."

"You don't owe me a version of yourself you're not ready for."

It was the one thing she hadn't expected to hear.

"I think," he added, "maybe I just needed to know I wasn't crazy. That it meant something. That I didn't imagine you."

"You didn't."

They stayed like that, breathing in sync but not speaking, softened into something companionable.

Outside, a siren passed. Inside, a shift, small but seismic. Nico glanced toward the door that connected their rooms.

"I hated that door," he said. "Every day you didn't knock."

She stood. Walked toward the connecting door. Opened it. The light spilled through. She turned back. "I'm ready now."

And left it open as she walked back to her room.

Chapter Twelve

THE MORNING AFTER DOESN'T LIE

The door was still ajar between their rooms. It had been for hours.
Nico hadn't closed it, and Sienna hadn't walked through it.
Until now.

She stepped over the threshold barefoot, breath held high in her chest, holding something back that had waited long enough. Nico was at the edge of his bed, shirt half buttoned, as if he hadn't decided whether to sleep or pace all night. They looked at each other without smiles or nerves - they just saw each other.

"I wasn't sure if you'd come," he said.
She shrugged. "I wasn't either."
She moved closer, standing just far enough away that he could change his mind. He didn't. His hand reached for hers, tentative, like he was afraid to startle her. Their fingers met, "You still run cold," he said, brushing his fingers across her wrist.
"You still state the obvious," she replied, not moving.
But then something shifted, an invisible nudge forward. Their bodies filled the space that their pride had held hostage for days. She moved first, closing the last inch.
His mouth met hers without hesitation, without a soundtrack. Skin on skin, breath caught between them, lips parting like it was inevitable. It wasn't hunger at first; it was permission and recognition.

Then his hand moved to her waist. Her fingers slid under the collar of his shirt. And that's when she laughed.

"What?" he asked, breath uneven.

"This shirt," she whispered. "Still smells like self-restraint."

He smiled. "It's clean."

"You're not."

"Neither are you."

She pushed the shirt off his shoulders. It caught awkwardly on one arm. They both chuckled, and the spell didn't break; it deepened.

She nudged his side after a slightly awkward adjustment. "Definitely not a perfect, high-budget film moment, is it?"

He smiled against her jaw. "It's better. It's ours."

She kissed him again, slower this time, anchoring herself in the feel of his lips. The memory of them. His hands moved up her back, cautious at first, like he was learning the new map of her.

Her dress had a hidden zip. Of course it did, mildly infuriating. His fingers found it with more hope than goals.

"Is it?" he started.

"Stuck," she said flatly.

He paused. "Should I…?"

"Just rip the damn thing off."

He laughed, a genuine, warm sound. "Ok."

He wrestled with it for a moment, muttering something that didn't sound flattering. The zip gave with a sigh, and the fabric slipped from her shoulders like it had been waiting.

"Thank God," she whispered. "Great in theory. Hell in practice."

His eyes lingered over her, like a second look that remembered the first. "Practice makes perfect."

She gave a shaky laugh. "I guess we need a lot more practice, then."

Nico ran a hand down her arm, his touch feather-light but charged. He moved slowly. Not like when they were young. He traced her collarbone, the dip at her waist, like every new line was something sacred.

His shirt hit the floor without resistance. Her dress had taken half a decade of emotional unpacking to remove. But now she stood in front of him bare, steady, unashamed.

His eyes never left hers.

"This isn't a redo," she said.

"I know."

"And it's not a promise."

"I know that too."

Their bodies met in a convergence instead of a crash. It was heat, yes, but it was also memory and forgiveness. It was hunger built over more than twenty years of pretending it didn't matter.

His mouth moved from her lips to her neck. Her hands gripped his back, pulling him closer, grounding herself there. Skin to skin, they reacquainted themselves with the shape of each other, and with everything they hadn't said.

She gasped once. He stilled. She didn't tell him to keep going. She showed him. Shifted under his weight, wrapped a leg around his hip, guided him in the way only a woman who knows her body, and wants to be known can.

It wasn't perfect. It wasn't choreographed. It was real. A shoulder bump. A laugh muffled into a kiss. The way she hissed when his stubble grazed too hard, and the way he immediately softened. He murmured something about her skin. She didn't reply. She pulled him closer.

This wasn't them in their twenties.

This was better.

They lay tangled in the hush of it. The kind of hush that doesn't beg to be filled. Only softened by breath and skin cooling against fabric.

Sienna stared at the ceiling, the familiar weight of overthinking tugging at her edges. But it hadn't won.

He reached for her hand, the tips of his fingers brushing hers, like he was still asking permission.

She turned to face him.

His eyes were open.

"I was scared I made you up," he said, voice hoarse.

"You didn't."

"You disappeared."

"I know."

He let the space breathe around the truth that had already been named.

She exhaled. Her body didn't feel used. It felt known. Seen, even in the dark. Especially in the dark.

"You ok?" he asked.

"I think I forgot what it felt like to not apologise for being here," she said.

Nico brushed across her knuckles.

They didn't say anything else. They didn't need to.

O—
TSR

Morning didn't ask for permission. She woke first. Pale light spilling in between the curtains. His back was to her; his arm draped across the pillow. His hair was messy. A faint crease between his brows, like even in sleep, he didn't fully let go.

She sat up.

Watched him.

Her chest ached, not from fear of being loved, but from the sharp, unexpected realisation that she might still want something from this. From him.

Love at this age didn't look like fireworks and declarations, even if you wanted it to, unless you were very, very lucky. It looked like wondering if she was daring enough to believe again. To trust herself not to vanish when it got too good. To stay.

"Don't do this," she whispered to herself. "Don't build a castle on one night."

And yet, she didn't move.

She watched him breathe.

She thought about the nights she'd spent alone, pretending solitude was a choice. About all the noise she'd made in her life to drown out the wanting.

She looked at the man beside her and wondered if maybe, this time, she didn't have to run.

He shifted slightly in his sleep and murmured her name. Softly. Like it lived in him still.

And in her bones, she felt the answer creeping in, uninvited.

She lay back down beside him, mirroring the curve of his spine with her own body's shape. Close, but not tethered. Her breath steadied, syncing with his, slower now, grounded. For a moment, it was enough just to exist in the same rhythm.

A bird chirped outside the window, one of those oddly hopeful morning sounds she used to resent. Now it felt like a dare.

Nico stirred, not fully waking, a subtle adjustment, like his body remembered she was there. His hand stretched across the mattress, fingers grazing her hip. She closed her eyes.

They didn't speak right away when he woke. She watched him take in the room, then her. No panic or post-mistake politeness. Only eyes that softened, and a small smile that meant *I'm still here.*

"I don't usually sleep well in hotels," he said, voice gravelled. "Last night... I did."

She smiled back, tight-lipped. "Could've been the sex."

He grinned, but it didn't deflect. "Could've been you."

That felt like the right answer. She sat up again, the sheet clinging to her waist, and reached for the coffee that hadn't been brewed, the stillness that hadn't been interrupted.

"Do we talk about it?" she asked.

He propped himself up on one elbow. "We can. Or we can just sit in it for a minute. Let it be real before we pick it apart."

That, somehow, felt like the most grown-up thing either of them had said all night.

"Ok," she whispered. "One minute."

The clock ticked. Somewhere down the hall, someone's door closed. Another life, another story. But this one, this room, this morning, felt like it still had something left to say.

She leaned over and kissed him. She wanted to confirm it had happened; she wasn't trying to recapture anything; she just wanted to make sure he was real and that she was too.

She stayed there beside him longer than she meant to. Absorbing the atmosphere like it was charged with something she hadn't felt in years, hope, maybe, danger, or both. It was terrifying to want something that didn't come with terms and conditions.

He shifted again and turned toward her, sleep still clouding his eyes, but no confusion in them.

"What are you thinking?" he asked.

She hesitated. Then: "That you still smell like your twenties and that's highly unfair."

He let out a low laugh, one that rumbled against her chest as he reached up to tuck a strand of hair behind her ear. "You're not the only one who remembers," he said. "It wasn't just summer. It wasn't just a story."

Her throat tightened.

"I tried to tell myself that," she whispered. "For years. That it was just a detour."

"What do you think it was now?"
"Now I'm wondering if it was the map."

He leaned in; he wanted to kiss her. Instead, he rested his forehead against hers. They stayed like that, breath to breath.
The ache inside her wasn't fear this time. It was recognition. Of herself. Of him. Of the space between them finally narrowing.

Chapter Thirteen

THE CONFERENCE SPEECH

The crowd inside was bustling, high heels on marble, glasses clinking, last-minute whispers about market trends and campaign reach. The air reeked of money, ego, and performative mentorship. Sienna had sat in those chairs for years. She'd taken notes. She'd played the game.

"I swear," Olivia muttered, balancing a mini crème brûlée on a cocktail napkin, "If one more guy talks about *the vision* while sweating through a polyester blazer, I'm going to stab myself with the tiny fork they gave us with dessert."

Sienna smirked. "It's called restraint. You're not supposed to inhale five courses and still have room for burnt cream."

"I'm a modern woman. I contain multitudes. Including dessert," Olivia said proudly.

Sienna grinned. "At least the catering's decent. I inhaled a $40 scallop."

"At least you did it in that dress. You're welcome, by the way. Clearly, I missed my calling," Olivia said, with the expression of someone accepting an award on behalf of taste itself.

Sienna glanced down at the dress Olivia had insisted she wear, deep plum, structured cut, subtle embellishments at the collar and elbows. It looked like money. The kind of money that doesn't need to raise its voice.

"I look like I'm about to launch a tech empire while sipping something with a verbena sprig," Sienna said.

"You look like you invoice in six figures and buy companies just to fire the HR department." Olivia giggled as they moved toward the stage.

Backstage was dim and buzzed with the usual mayhem, crew members darting around with earpieces and clipboards, assistants muttering updates, someone panic rehearsing a speech about brand agility. A young staffer scurried over with a remote. Sienna looked at it like it was a loaded weapon.

Back there, it was colder than expected. It wasn't the temperature itself; it was the tone, clinical, sterile, too far from the glow of the lounge, from last night's skin-on-skin confessions. Her heels clicked softly against the floor as she paced. The screen in front of her displayed the first slide of her presentation: title, subtitle, clean lines. Safe.

Sienna hated safe.

She clutched the cue cards in one hand, the remote in the other. They felt like props for a version of her she no longer recognised.

Olivia had her arms crossed, one brow arched like she was ready to throw the cards in the nearest bin herself. "Don't you dare walk out there and give them TED Talk Barbie."

Sienna gave a dry laugh. "That was never the plan."

"But it's the backup plan."

She held Olivia's gaze. It wasn't just a look. It was a silent dare. A push. The kind of look only your best friend can deliver without saying a word: *Tell the truth. Or don't bother speaking.*

Sienna looked down at her hands. The remote. The cue cards.

The neat deck waiting on the screen behind her.

She thought about last night. Nico's mouth on her skin. The way he hadn't rushed her. The way she'd seen herself in his eyes, messy, flawed, radiant. Her throat tightened. It was still there, in her bloodstream. In her breath.

She didn't want to pitch. She wanted to purge.

She tossed the cue cards on the bench and pressed the remote once, off.

"No slides?" Olivia asked, mildly impressed.

"No slides," Sienna confirmed.

"You're all set," the assistant chirped.

"I'm not using slides," Sienna said.

The assistant blinked. "Sorry?"

"No slides. No remote. No bullet points. Me, and only me."

Olivia snorted from behind a curtain. "Cue the fainting."

The staffer nodded, looking confused. She scurried off, visibly rethinking her life choices and muttering about *updating the program.*

Sienna exhaled and smoothed the front of her dress.

"You sure about this?" Olivia asked.

"No."

"Perfect."

Sienna gave her a small, sharp smile. "If I tank, you're buying the drinks."

"Oh, honey," Olivia said, eyes sparkling, "I'm buying champagne either way."

Sienna exhaled and squared her shoulders.

As she stepped toward the curtain, her voice steady, her spine taller than it had been in years, she muttered more to herself than to Olivia: "We've all sat through a hundred of these. Bullet points. Bar graphs. Case studies that sound more like alibis than the real truth. But today… I don't want to show them a strategy. I want to show them what it looks like to burn it down and begin again."

She thought: *Let's see what happens when the woman with the mic stops reading from a script made by others.*

The emcee's voice echoed through the ballroom: "And now, to close this year's summit, a woman who needs no introduction, though she's probably rewritten hers twice this week, a woman whose campaigns didn't just make waves, they changed the current. Please welcome Sienna Hartley."

Applause rolled out like a slow-building swell.

Sienna stepped forward, head high. The spotlight caught her, and in that moment, she didn't think about Marc, Nico or failure.

The second Sienna Hartley stepped up to the mic, there was a shift; the lean forward, the quieting of utensils and the throat-clears began. The giant screen behind her was blank.

"Good morning.

Don't worry, I'm not here to sell you anything. No graphs. No buzzwords. Just a woman with a microphone and a midlife crisis."

Scattered chuckles. A few exchanged glances. She paced and let the sound settle before speaking again.

"I know what you were expecting," she said, her voice even but lagging. "A keynote about market share. Brand alignment."

She took a breath, her voice dipping, honest now. Exposed, yet steady.

"This isn't the speech I planned. I was meant to be standing here showing you a case study. I even had slides. There was a quote from Maya Angelou that I definitely stole from Pinterest. That one had bullet points and a few lines that would've made my old creative director cry happy tears. But then something happened. I scrapped it. It just didn't feel right because none of it felt true."

The audience shifted again. Less amused now, curious and more alert. She took a breath.

"And I think that's the problem, isn't it? We get so good at polishing stories, we forget how to tell them. So, here's mine."

"I'm forty-eight. And this year, I realised I was still introducing myself with a resume from ten years ago and a personality I'd outgrown.

I'd stayed loyal to a version of myself that stopped being real years ago."

A few mm-hmms. Heads nodding.

"I think we call that something else. The cost of wasted time. Of being who you thought they wanted, instead of who you needed to be."

She paused because she felt it all and knew she had to go on without the feeling of overwhelm taking over.

"I'd built a career on voice. Crafting it, curating it, polishing it until it sounded like certainty. But I'd forgotten my own. I'd forgotten that reinvention doesn't require permission. It just needs proof you are alive and willing."

More nods now. Stillness.

"Last year, I stood in the bathroom at my old office, staring at a version of myself I didn't recognise. Hair perfectly positioned. Red lipstick worn like a mask of confidence. Eyes tired. I had the job, the marriage, the apartment with the hardwood floors and the expensive art on the walls.

And I was miserable.

Not because of one big thing, but because of a thousand tiny ones. The kind of things that chip away at you so subtly, you don't realise how much you've given away until there's nothing to come home to.

You know that feeling?

When you start saying 'I'm fine' like it's a reflex.

When you shrink a little to make room for someone else's ambition.

When your own name sounds foreign in your mouth because you haven't heard it said with love in years."

She paused. No one moved.

"I left it all.

I didn't leave gracefully, and not with a five-year plan. I left with a bag, a bank account that barely covered what it cost to leave, and a voice in my head that said, *You can't come back from this.* And maybe that voice was right. Maybe the woman I was doesn't exist anymore.

But the one standing here does. And she's not sorry.

I've learned that reinvention isn't always a transformation. Sometimes it's a breakdown in a hotel room. A friend telling you the truth when you don't want to hear it. A night with someone who remembers who you were, before the revisions. Before the compromises.

Reinvention is ugly. And liberating. And late. And sometimes, exactly on time."

Sienna walked across the stage. Her dress caught the light as she moved.

"Here's what I know:

We spend a lot of time in this industry talking about authenticity. *Be real.' 'Be bold.' 'Be disruptive.'* But half the time, we don't even mean it. We mean be just real enough to sell the thing. Be bold, but not too loud. Be disruptive - but don't rock the boat if the client's in the room.

But what if the client's waiting for us to be brave?

What if people don't want another pitch? What if they want to feel something?"

She scanned the room. Let her voice drop just slightly.

"I've sat in hundreds of rooms like this. You have too. Rooms full of smart, tired people pretending not to be falling apart. And here's what I wish someone had told me five years ago:

You don't need to be more productive. You need to be more *alive.*

The best work I've done in my career didn't come from being on top of everything. It came from being on the edge of myself. It came from choosing honesty over being perfect. It came from knowing that fear is not a stop sign; it's a signpost

So, if you're waiting for permission to make a mess, take a risk, burn it down and begin again, this is it."

A murmur. Then stillness. Her words landed like confetti and bricks all at the same time.

"I'm not the woman I was a year ago. I don't even think I'm the woman I was yesterday.

But I'm *here now.*

And that counts for something.

So instead of showing you bullet points and ROI stats, I'll tell you this: Whatever you're holding onto, whatever version of success you were taught to chase. Ask yourself, who is it serving? And if it's not *you,* if it's not *true,* let it go.

Reinvention isn't failure. It's evolution. And yes, it's absolutely terrifying. But it's also the most honest kind of freedom you will ever have."

Sienna stepped back from the mic a little. Then returned.

"You know what takes courage? Not jumping out of planes or pitching to billion-dollar clients. Courage is looking at your life and saying, 'That chapters done. I'm not pretending anymore; it is time for me to be alive.'"

Someone clapped. Somcone else shushed them.

She smiled.

"Starting again when no one's cheering, that's where the story gets good. When no one's watching. No one's liking your work. When you leave the job, or the marriage, or the version of yourself that made everyone else comfortable, and you sit in the aftermath and say, 'Ok. Now what?'"

Her eyes scanned the room.

"And if you're lucky... You find out that underneath everything you performed, there's still someone worth listening to. Worth trusting. Worth following, even if she's just walking out of a hotel room, wondering if her life still fits."

Another pause.

She looked up.

"Sometimes the story doesn't end. It just waits until you're ready to finish writing it."

There was something in her tone. It wasn't sadness, maybe a trace of someone she used to know, a flicker of someone she might still love?

"I'm not here to tell you how to build a brand that wins. You already know how to do that. You've done it. I'm just here to remind you that sometimes the boldest campaign you'll ever run... is the one where you stop selling and start becoming."
"Oh, and one last thing."
She grinned. Olivia would be proud.
"If your next keynote speaker shows up with a remote and a graph, ask them when they last changed their life. Because that's the only data point that matters."

She stepped back from the mic. She didn't say thank you, she didn't show them a close-out slide, she left them with honesty.
It was almost reverent. Like the room had collectively forgotten how to breathe.
Then - applause. Not the kind you get out of obligation. It started slowly from somewhere near the middle. Then it swelled, folding across the rows like a tide.
Sienna waited there for a second too long. Absorbing. She'd spoken the truth out loud, and it hadn't swallowed her whole.
As she stepped down from the stage, a woman in the third row wiped her cheek and gave a small, stunned nod. Behind her, a man looked like someone had just pulled the rug out from under his perfectly structured trend analysis graph.
A tall woman in sharp camel tailoring intercepted her with a business card and a sentence that started with, "We need to talk." Something about a global agency. Something about creative lead. Sienna didn't quite catch it. Not all of it. Her pulse was still rushing in her ears.
Olivia was suddenly there, slipping in beside her.
"You just changed your life," she whispered. Then, without missing a beat: "And stole mine, bitch. I was meant to be the emotional one."

Sienna half-laughed, half-exhaled. "You'll manage. You always do; it's one of the many reasons why I love you."

"You'd better hope I do. Because when you panic later and pretend you didn't mean any of it, I'm the one who's going to talk you out of fleeing to Iceland."

They moved toward the exit, the noise of the room not quite reaching her. The lights. The people. The cards and compliments. It was all background.

Because her heart was beating harder than it had all day, and not because of the stage. Not even because of the offer. It was because, for the first time in too long, everything that came next would be hers to choose.

And the strongest thing she did wasn't standing up there.

It was what she didn't say.

What she still hadn't said.

Chapter Fourteen

THE OFFER

The applause chased them down the hall. Olivia grabbed her hand, guiding her toward the lift, but it was too late.

They were already waiting. Polished people in expensive fabrics with hungry eyes.

"You were incredible."

"Do you have a rep?"

"We should talk soon."

Business cards appeared like magic. Compliments disguised as lock-in contracts. Sienna was still caught in the afterglow, not sure if she was flattered or hunted.

"Excuse me?"

She turned.

A woman mid-twenties, wearing a conference lanyard and mascara like war paint, stood a few feet away. She was uncertain but propelled by something urgent.

"I just wanted to say… thank you. For saying what nobody else would. That thing about rewriting the story?" Her voice wavered. "I needed that."

"Thank you," Sienna said, her voice slower than usual, like it had to wade through too much feeling to get out clean.

The woman nodded once, fast. "You reminded me I'm allowed to want more," she added.

Sienna noticed a chipped nail on her pinky. Something so human it undid her a little.

And then she was gone, swallowed by the crowd. A blur of tailored suits and structured interest, all armed with smooth smiles and LinkedIn-ready pitches. They'd seen her speak and heard the shift in her voice, the unscripted sincerity, the raw power of someone who wasn't trying to impress anymore. And they wanted to bottle it. Sell it. Use it.

It was time to vacate; she grabbed Olivia's arm and bolted to the lifts. She pressed the lift button with a steady hand and waited.

When the doors opened to their floor, Sienna exhaled, and the thoughts that followed felt louder than the applause echoing in her head.

By the time she returned to her hotel suite, her inbox had thirty-two new messages. Half subject lined: "Incredible speech." The other half: "Opportunity."

She ignored them all.

She tossed her shoes into a corner, took off her earrings that still smelled like old nerves and stage lights, and positioned herself in the centre of the room as if it had shifted while she was gone. Maybe it had. Everything felt very different now.

Her phone lit up.

Marc.

Can we try again, dinner? One last toast to your triumph. My treat. No speeches, promise.

She stared at the message for a moment longer than she wanted to admit. Then she typed:

Fine. One drink.

TSR

The restaurant was glossy. Upscale in that intentional, sterile way that made everyone look better in low lighting.

Marc was already there; his success wore him, not the other way around. When he stood to greet her, he held her gaze just long enough to test the waters.

"You were magnificent," he said, sliding into his chair like this was still their rhythm. "Commanding. Poised. You always had that in you, but tonight…" He raised his glass. "Tonight, you reminded the room."

She didn't toast back.

"I didn't do it for the room," she said coolly.

He laughed, unbothered. "Of course not. But you can't blame the room for wanting more."

The menu sat untouched between them. She didn't need to open it to know he'd already pre-ordered their wine. The exact one she used to drink again, back when she still thought saying "I'll have what he's having" made her seem elegant, not erased.

He poured for her without asking.

Old habits. Annoying.

"So," she said, resting a single hand on the menu without looking at it. "You've rehearsed this."

Marc smiled, like they were in on a private joke. "I've been talking to a few people in London. High-end agency. Global campaigns, prestige clients. They saw the speech. They saw you. And they're interested."

"In me?" she said flatly.

"In us," he said, too quickly.

And there it was.

She watched him watching her. His eyes lingered not with admiration, but calculation, like she was a property that had regained value.

Something to be acquired. Flipped.

"Your name's back in the right rooms, Sienna. You've never been more valuable."

She tried not to raise her eyebrow and glare, feeling the harsh emptiness of it all.

She stared at him. It wasn't the offer that unsettled her. It was how easy it was to forget, even for a second, that this used to be flattering.

Marc leaned in. "You've got a second chance to own the world we built. Together. What do you say?"

She now felt the air was strangling her, and the moment, and finally…

"You never saw me, did you?" she said, voice level. "You just knew how to market me for your own gain."

"I say," she replied, "I built it. You just branded it."

Marc registered the hit.

And with that, she walked out, deciding she was never going back.

Sienna headed to the bar to wash off the feeling that she'd brushed up against something she didn't want to carry home. It was empty, except for a woman with a martini and an air of indifference that Sienna instantly respected.

She ordered a drink, sat by the window, and pulled out her phone. She didn't text Nico, although she wanted to; instead, she opened a message from Olivia she'd left unread earlier.

"Are you floating or falling? Also, if Marc says, "second chance" one more time, I'll fly in and drown him in artisanal gin."

Sienna smiled. Then she dialled.

Olivia answered on the first ring.

"Tell me you didn't go to dinner with the ex-husband-shaped leech."

"One drink on neutral ground."

"I hope it was poison," Olivia stated.

Sienna laughed.

"He offered me London," she said, eyes flicking to the skyline.

A pause. Then Olivia's voice lowered.

"Let me guess. Big agency. Global campaigns. An office with a view and a leash disguised as a necklace."

Sienna didn't answer.

"I know what that looks like, Si," Olivia said gently. "I know how much you used to want it."

"I did want it," Sienna murmured.

"Yeah. When you still thought freedom came in black folders and signed contracts."

"So," Olivia asked finally. "What do *you* want now?"

Sienna stared out the window. The city pulsed, alive and disinterested.

"I want to want something real," she said.

"So what's your big next thing?" Sienna asked, mostly to deflect.

Olivia's laugh was quick but thinner than usual. "There's a contract in London, coincidentally. Six months. Supposed to be career-defining."

"You'd actually leave?" Sienna asked.

"Maybe. Maybe not." A pause crackled down the line. "Guess I'll find out if I'm as brave as I keep telling you to be."

Sienna smiled into the silence. "You already are."

TSR

The hotel suite felt too subdued. That kind of calm that gets under your skin; it wasn't peace, but something more accusing. Sienna turned on the light, only to turn it off again. The glow made everything look too soft and too forgiving, and she didn't want soft. She wanted honesty. She poured herself a glass of wine, sat on the edge of the bed, and stared at the window, hoping the city might offer answers if she looked long enough. Lights flickered, cabs moved, stories unfolded in rooms just like this one, but none of them were hers.

Her phone buzzed again.

This time, it was a message from Nico.

"If you're still here… I'd like to talk."

She stared at the screen like it might pulse, because her pulse was beating hard.

It was almost worse than no message at all. The restraint of it. The lack of demand.

Was he trying to win? Was he just showing up? Was this… normal? Sienna was so used to manipulation that she dissected everything, every sentence, every word, as if it came with conditions.

A knock at the door made her jump. Room service? She hadn't ordered anything.

She padded barefoot to the door and peered through the peephole. No one was there. But something had been slid under the door.

An envelope.

Cream-coloured, no hotel branding, just her name in neat black ink.

Inside was a single sheet of heavy card. An invitation. She quickly dropped it on the floor.

She stared at it for a while, unsure if she wanted to read it; it could be from Nico. Or worse, from Marc. Another ploy, a letter laced with apology and his ego plastered all over it. *Why won't he stop and let me go?*

Her pulse quickened in anticipation laced with dread. She crouched, picked it up, and read the first line once.

Then again.

Deliciae Private Portfolio Invitation - For Your Eyes Only.

A personalised pitch from the very agency Marc had name-dropped. Except… it wasn't Marc who sent it. It was someone else, someone who *had* watched her speech, who had found it "disarming, fierce, and unsettling in the best way." It was a compliment. A genuine one. And yet, she still couldn't shake the chill of being watched. She looked around her suite.

You're formally invited to step back into your power. You already did the hard part; you told the truth. Now you get to decide who hears it next.

Her shoulders tensed. The muscles along her spine tightened like someone had just placed a hand between her shoulder blades.
At the bottom:

Deliciae International - Executive Creative Consultant Offer
Location: London, New York, or Anywhere You Want

She exhaled through her nose. A long, steady breath, she didn't realise she'd been holding.
She stared at it. Anywhere you want…
It was supposed to sound like freedom. But it reeked of seduction. The handpicked kind. The kind with fine print that stifled you softly.
She folded it once. Then again. And dropped it on the desk. Same room. Same view. A different woman was standing in it.
Maybe the point wasn't what she chose next.
Maybe the point was that it would be hers alone?

⚷
TSR

That night, she was standing on the hotel rooftop. Alone. The air smelled faintly of mint. Below her, the city was still pulsing, but she didn't feel lost in it anymore.
She felt… momentarily unmoored.
She took a breath, typed a reply to Nico's message:
"I'm still here. But I'm not running this time. I'm thinking."
Before she could hit send, she heard a voice behind her.
"Thinking looks good on you."

She turned. It wasn't Nico.

It was Harper. The concierge. The woman always seemed to know too much and say too little.

"I'm off duty," Harper said with a small smile. "Thought I'd borrow the view."

Sienna watched her, unsure what to say.

Harper looked out across the skyline, then said, "You know, we get all kinds through these doors. People who come to escape, to celebrate, to vanish."

"And me?" Sienna asked.

"You came to decide."

A pause.

Then Harper added, her voice softer now, less concierge, more confidante:

"You think you need direction. But maybe you just need a door that opens inward."

"But what if I open the wrong one?" Sienna asked.

Harper smiled faintly, already turning to go.

"Then you'll know something you didn't before."

"But for what it's worth…" Harper added, "You don't need a new city. You just need a new room."

She walked away with a grin. As she reached the stairs, she glanced back.

It wasn't a look of curiosity.

It was recognition.

Sienna remained after Harper disappeared down the stairs, the air shifting behind her like a door closing softly.

She turned back to the skyline. The city wasn't beautiful tonight; it was *bare*. Brutal, alive, unfiltered. And for the first time, she didn't feel like she needed to keep up with it. She could just… *be in it.*

She glanced down at her phone again.

"I'm still here. But I'm not running this time. I'm thinking."

She stared at the message. It was true. But it wasn't necessary.

She tapped Select All. Then Delete.

The screen returned to empty. No dots. No expectations.

She slid the phone into her pocket and moved toward the edge of the rooftop, resting both hands on the cool metal railing. The wind picked up and tangled through her hair. A plane blinked overhead.

Somewhere, below, someone was laughing too loudly, and for once, it didn't pierce her.

She didn't need to be seen to feel real.

She didn't need to be answered to feel steady.

The world wasn't waiting for her to choose.

She was the choice.

TSR

The next morning, she called Olivia again. This time from the bath.

"I got another offer," she said, blowing into the receiver like the steam might disguise her ambivalence.

"Let me guess. More money, more flattery, more soul-leasing?"

"They called me a disrupter. Said I'm 'un-brandable in the best way.'"

Olivia laughed. "That's corporate code for 'we have no idea what to do with her, but she's trending.'"

"I used to want this," Sienna said.

"You used to want to disappear into it," Olivia corrected. "Now you want to emerge from it. Big difference."

They were the kind of friends who've already said everything but keep the line open anyway.

Finally, Olivia said, "Do you want me to tell you what you already know?"

"Always."

"You don't need them anymore. You don't need *him*. You didn't get
here because of Marc. You got here despite him. You don't owe him a
callback. You owe *yourself* a clean start."

Sienna swirled her fingers in the water.

A clean start.

What did that even look like now?

She spent the afternoon walking the city alone. Not because she was
searching but because she needed to remember what it felt like to
choose her own pace.

She ducked into a gallery. Wandered aisles of moody portraiture.

Paused at a photograph: a woman, maybe forty, walking away from the
camera in a red coat. Her face unseen, but something in her posture
was defiant and tired and free, hit hard.

It wasn't her. But it *could* have been.

On the way back to the hotel, she passed a bookstore. Without
thinking, she stepped inside. Browsed poetry. Bought a slim volume by
a writer she once loved and hadn't thought of in years.

Back in the suite, she opened to a random page.

"You are not who they remember.

You are who you decide to become,

when no one is watching."

She let the words settle.

Maybe this was the whole point: not reinvention. Not reclamation.

But emergence.

Chapter Fifteen

THE PAST REWRITTEN

Sienna stepped inside the suite like she was walking into a room she hadn't felt the right to be in. The door clicked shut behind her, soft as a secret. Olivia had peeled off two floors down with a half-formed sentence about drinks and needing to call her sister. A pretext, obviously. The kind people used when what they were really offering was space, and Sienna had let her go. She wasn't in the mood to be witnessed.

The lounge door was shut.

It had only ever been closed twice before. Once, when Nico had arrived. Again, when he'd retreated after she pushed too hard with too little. This made three. And it felt worse than before. More decisive. Final.

She walked across the suite; the air felt dense and saturated, like the room itself had absorbed too much emotion and was now holding it in protest. She opened the door to the lounge and crossed over to his door. She paused, knocked once, nothing.

She tried the handle. It turned easily. Effortless. The way some departures were.

His suite was empty.

And it was painfully, deliberately neat.

No boots by the wall. No shirt tossed over the back of a chair. No trace
of the scuffed passport he carried like a lucky charm. No books. No
glass half-drunk and forgotten on the edge of a table. Only... absence.
She closed her eyes and could see him anyway, the slope of his
shoulders filling a doorway, casual but impossibly certain, as though
leaning there was enough to claim the space.
Even the scent, that clean masculine note she could identify in a crowd,
was faint now. Evaporating.
The curtains were pulled halfway, letting in strips of white morning
light that made everything too visible. The bed had been made. Not like
housekeeping makes it. Like a person who cared about how they left
things. A ritual of exit.
Her eyes caught on the desk.
One upside-down coffee cup. Washed. Dried. Placed carefully on its
saucer.
She stepped forward. Reached out. Her fingers skimmed the varnished
wood and caught on the faint ring left by an earlier cup. She
remembered the way he'd rest his hand there too, long fingers
drumming absently, veins tracing up toward a wrist she'd once kissed in
the dark.
Proof of him.
Proof he had been here. That she'd had him close enough to touch,
speak, mess up with, and now he was gone.
The ache was dull. Spreading a heaviness that settled behind her ribs
and refused to leave.
She turned in a slow circle. Scanning the room for anything he might've
missed. A note. A trace. A strand of hair. Something.
But the room was spotless. Clean in the way people clean when they're
trying to erase themselves gently.
Back in her own suite, the contrast hit. The bed unmade. Her coat
draped over a chair. A pair of heels on their side near the desk, like

they'd collapsed. A half-finished bottle of perfume sitting at an odd angle, the cap off.

It looked like someone had left in a hurry and forgotten to actually go.

Then she saw it.

An envelope. Neatly placed on the console near the wall with a name. SIENNA.

The sight of it made her stomach tilt.

She stared at it. She felt something rising in her chest, resistance, maybe. Or grief. Or the haunting suggestion of possibility.

Instead, she moved to the minibar.

Opened it. Grabbed the first bottle within reach. Poured it into a glass without checking the label, without ice or tonic, delivering a harsh bite. She sipped.

And yet, nothing burned as much as nothing. She walked back to the couch. Sat down like the weight of the air had caught up with her. Glass in one hand. Envelope in the other.

She turned it over. Ran her fingers across the handwriting.

That same all-caps scrawl. She'd seen it before, scribbled on napkins, in the margins of postcards, on the note he'd left at the foot of a Spanish church twenty-six years ago. That one she'd burned without reading. She could still smell the acrid curl of paper on a Barcelona balcony, the night air heavy with jasmine and smoke. She could still see it now, the square outside that church, heat shimmering off cobblestones, tourists drifting past while she stayed frozen in the shadowed arch. She hadn't said goodbye. Just watched the air waiver and carry her choice into silence.

She didn't know if she wished she had read it until now.

She opened the envelope.

Sienna,

I once told you I don't like rewriting history. That I prefer to let things sit where they fell.

I lied.

I've rewritten you in my head a hundred different ways. Angry. Distant. Brave. Heartbroken. In none of them did you tell me why you left. And in all of them, I still wanted you.

I came back here thinking I could make peace with it. With you.

I didn't come looking for closure; I don't believe in it. I came looking for the truth.

You didn't owe me then. But maybe you owe yourself now.

You said once that the past doesn't have to define us. That we get to decide who we are. If that's true, then let this be the moment you choose to remember us differently.

I won't wait. That's not what this is.

But if you want to find me, really find me, you already know where to look.

N.

She sat frozen.

The glass tilted in her hand, forgotten.

He hadn't said goodbye. He hadn't given her a roadmap. He hadn't begged or blamed.

He'd simply left.

A clean sentence. A mirror held up. A dare dressed as permission.

She read it again.

The line that undid her was the simplest:

You didn't owe me then. But maybe you owe yourself now.

She didn't know how long she sat like that.

Minutes. Maybe hours. The city outside blurred into ambient noise, cars and sirens and someone shouting two floors below. The thrum of a place that did not care whether two people loved or lost each other inside a hotel.

She set the letter down carefully on the coffee table.

Got up. Walked to the window.

The city glared back at her, bright and indifferent. Yellow cabs. Glinting rooftops. Someone was jogging across the avenue in leggings that cost more than her shoes. People moved. Lived. Decided.

And she stood still.

Her reflection in the glass stared back. She looked exhausted. Pale, emptied. And beneath the exhaustion, something else.

Recognition.

The woman in the glass was her. But not the version she presented to clients or on stages or in glossy marketing reels. This was the woman who had left Nico in Barcelona with no explanation.

This was the woman who never quite stopped remembering him, even when she couldn't admit it aloud.

She pressed her palm to the glass, then pulled away. A mark remained. Temporary. Like presence. Like memory.

She walked to the desk. Sat. Turned the lamp on.

Pulled out the journal and began to write.

She didn't know what she was writing at first. Her hand moved before she caught up to the words. They spilled onto the page like they'd been waiting. It wasn't a letter or a journal entry. It was the truth, in fragments.

I left because I didn't trust what was real.
Because you didn't make promises, and I didn't know how to believe in anything without one.
Because loving you felt too fragile to hold.

She paused.

The pen hovered, then returned to the paper.

I spent years mastering distance. Perfecting control. I thought if I could name it, schedule it, and outwork it, I could survive it. I thought grief was something I could catalogue. But you were the one thing I couldn't manage.

She sat back in the chair. Let the pen fall.

Her fingers were trembling. Maybe it wasn't sadness. At least, not the kind she had a name for. This was something else. Older. Deeper.

She reached for the glass again, but this time, she didn't drink. She held it and let the condensation cool her palm.

She looked at what she'd written.

None of it sounded cultured. It wasn't the kind of confession you'd say out loud. But it was honest. And it was hers.

For a moment, she considered tearing the page out.

She did, and then she folded it.

She didn't wrap it tightly or hide it; she folded it once, down the centre. Like a breath.

She slid it into the back of her journal and closed the cover.

The letter from Nico still sat where she'd left it. But it no longer felt like a question.

She walked to the window again. The sky was starting to shift, grey giving way to something warmer, golden at the edges. The city was beginning its rehearsal for the morning. Delivery vans. Joggers. Streetlights blinking off, one by one.

Sienna touched the glass again.

This time, she didn't move from the window, not for a long time. Letting her fingers rest against the glass, she watched the world begin again. A man on a bicycle weaved between traffic. A florist rolled up a metal shutter. A girl in a school uniform waited at a crosswalk with her hair in two uneven braids and a neon green backpack that flashed with LEDs.

And Sienna, still barefoot, the hotel floor cool beneath her skin.

The grief didn't come in waves. It came in pauses. In remembering the sound of his voice saying her name and realising how few people ever said it without expectation.

She walked away from the window, feeling each step like it mattered.

There was no breakdown; there was a clean, internal fracture. A knowing.

He was gone.

And maybe, for the first time, she didn't want to run from what that meant.

She moved back into the bedroom and opened her suitcase. It was still half-packed, half-ignored. Shirts slumped over one side. A pair of trousers folded too quickly. The black shoes were tucked in the corner, exactly where she'd left them. She sat cross-legged on the floor and began to repack them with care, not because she had somewhere to be, but because the motion soothed her.

She found the top she'd worn the night they'd first spoken again. The one he'd touched absentmindedly while asking if she always looked like she'd just walked out of a vintage editorial. It still smelled faintly of hotel soap and her skin. Her body remembered more than her mind wanted to: his hand at her elbow that night, steadying her as she turned, the roughness of skin brushing silk. She had almost leaned in then, as if gravity itself belonged to him.

She pressed it to her face. Inhaled. Then folded it and slid it into her bag.

She wasn't sure if she was staying or leaving. But she knew she couldn't stay in this exact state. Frozen and waiting. Caught between action and inflexibility.

The journal still sat on the desk; the folded page tucked into the back. She didn't open it again. She didn't need to re-read her own honesty. It had been enough to finally write it.

She opened her laptop.

Paused.

Typed "Barcelona weather" into the search bar.

Then erased it. She wasn't ready to decide. But something was shifting.

Her phone vibrated softly beside her, startling her. She hadn't noticed the time. The messages from Olivia were stacking up now:

"Still at the bar downstairs if you need me."

"Just checking in."

"Do NOT pretend you're fine."

She smiled faintly.

Another buzz. A new one.

Marc.

"I saw the photos from the conference. You looked incredible."

"We should talk. Not about work."

She locked the screen without replying. She had no space for people who didn't know what they wanted until they saw someone else did.

She closed the messages and placed the phone face down.

There were too many versions of her people wanted access to: Sienna, the leader, the strategist, the ex, the friend who always had it together. And somewhere between all of them, the woman who wrote that page last night had slipped through the cracks.

She moved to the bathroom and turned on the tap.

The sound of water steadied her. She washed her face and deliberately, meaning to clear not just makeup or sleep, but also the lingering effects of the day. It felt like rinsing off the past twenty-six years. Or at least, the parts she'd let calcify.

She looked at her reflection. Still familiar. But not quite the same anymore.

She didn't look younger or older. She looked... returned, like someone who'd been out of her body and had finally come back to it.

A knock at the door pulled her from the mirror.

Three soft raps.

Another knock.

She stepped softly through the suite and peered through the peephole. Olivia.

Sienna opened the door.

Her friend, holding two takeaway coffees and a brown paper bag. Hair a mess, no makeup, her usual force of nature energy toned down to something easy and ready.

"I brought back up," Olivia said gently. "And carbs."

Sienna stepped aside.

Olivia placed the food on the counter, handed her one of the coffees, and waited.

They sat on the couch, the letter between them, unread by Olivia but heavy in the space all the same.

Sienna took a sip. The warmth helped. Or maybe the gesture did.

"I wrote something last night," she said softly.

Olivia looked at her. "Did you?"

Yeah." Sienna looked down at her glass. "Not for him. For me."

Olivia didn't respond with a cheer or a joke. She just nodded once, seriously, like that was the most grown-up thing she'd ever heard.

After a while, Sienna said, "He left."

"I figured."

There was a long pause. Then Olivia asked, "What are you going to do?"

Sienna looked down at the letter. Then at the journal where her own truth was folded and buried. And then, finally, at the city through the window, its stubborn insistence on carrying on.

"I'm not sure yet."

"That's allowed."

They sat for a while. Eating. Breathing. Drinking coffee. Existing.

And then Olivia got up.

"I'm going to shower and pretend I slept. You?"

"I might book a flight."

Olivia raised her brow. "Where to?"

"I don't know."

Olivia gave her a look, half smirk, half awe. "That might be the most honest thing you've ever said."

She disappeared into the second bathroom.

Sienna was alone again, but it felt different this time. She did not feel abandoned, she did not feel isolated, she felt still with room inside it.

She moved to her laptop. Opened the browser.

Typed: "One-way flights to Barcelona." The words felt like a key, unlocking a corner of memory, the tiled square where he'd bought her peaches, juice sticky down her wrist, the city's sunlight too merciless to lie beneath. A café, too bright with morning, him insisting she try the espresso black. No sugar, no milk. She'd pulled a face at the bitter edge, and he'd laughed, low, easy, as if the whole city was an acquired taste she might one day learn to love.

She paused.

Then added: "Leaving tonight."

Two seats remained on the late evening flight.

She stared at them.

Then clicked one.

And booked it.

She had no certainty, she had no hope, but she was full of readiness. She closed the laptop, reached for her suitcase, and finally zipped it shut; she glanced toward the bathroom. The shower was still running. Olivia hadn't said anything; she never did when she knew the goodbye was already happening.

She had one hand resting on the suitcase handle, as if waiting for something, confirmation, interruption, a sign from the universe that she'd done the right thing. Nothing came. The room remained as it was. The light through the window now golden, more forgiving than the clinical morning glare. Time had shifted. She had too. Not in some, life-altering way. But internally. The way landscapes change when no one's looking.

She walked over to the window again, this time opening it slightly, enough to let the city air inside. It smelled like rain on concrete and diesel and something sweet from the bakery below. Real life.

Her life.

Or maybe the life she hadn't let herself have. She placed her phone on the sill, opened the voice recorder, and stared at it. She didn't usually leave voice notes. She wrote and planned and cultivated. Her world was built in strategy decks and perfectly structured emails. But this wasn't for work. She hit record.

"Hi," she said. Then paused. *"This is not for you. Or maybe it is. But I need to say this somewhere, and right now, I can't say it to your face."*

She inhaled, then exhaled through her nose.

"I think I've spent my whole adult life outrunning moments like this. Choices I couldn't unmake. Things I didn't understand until too late. I told myself it was survival. I made it look like ambition."

She walked to the coffee table, still recording.

"But I left because I didn't believe someone like you could stay. And I didn't think I could survive the version of myself I'd have to become if you did. I thought it would make me smaller. Needy and weak."

A bitter laugh.

"And the truth is, you made me more unafraid than anyone ever had. You didn't save me. You didn't promise me a fairytale. You saw me. And that scared the hell out of me."

She sat on the edge of the couch.

"So, I'm flying to Barcelona tonight. Not to chase you or to even to see you, necessarily, well..... I'm going because I want to know who I am on the other side of the choices I never gave myself the chance to revisit."

A long pause.

"I don't know if this message is for you. But I think it's the first thing I've said in years that's actually for me."

She ended the recording. Didn't play it back and didn't delete it either. She saved it. Then took one last look around the suite, and whispered, "Let's rewrite this."

And walked out.

The hallway was hushed in that expensive-hotel way, thick carpet, soundproofed doors, dim sconces. Her boots made no sound as she walked, suitcase in tow. For once, the quiet didn't feel ominous.

At the elevator, she pressed the button and stared at her reflection in the mirrored doors. This time, not glamorous or composed, but sure. As the lift descended, she didn't scroll through her phone. Didn't check the flight confirmation. Didn't re-read the letter or her recording. She let it all breathe.

While Sienna was at the window, Olivia did what she always did best: moved, quickly, and with intention. She slipped out of the suite, bolted to the café, and tucked a note into the outer pocket of the bag.
The note read:
You'll never actually be late to your life. Go.

When Sienna reached the lobby, Olivia was waiting in the far corner, holding a pastry bag and a look that said, *I knew you'd go.*
Sienna gave her a small nod and a smile. Olivia was always there, especially when it mattered most. Nothing was explained between the two.

Outside, a cab pulled up. The driver stepped out and opened the trunk without a word. She handed him the case, climbed into the back seat, and gave the address.
JFK.
She unfolded the note in the back of the cab. It was exactly the kind of sentence Olivia would leave behind, pointed, true, and already in motion. And for the first time in what felt like decades, she didn't need to rehearse who she was or why she was going.
She was already becoming her on the way.

Chapter Sixteen

THE FIGHT

She found him in Barcelona.

It wasn't through a mutual contact or by chance. It was by instinct, the kind you don't admit to following because it makes you sound unhinged or hopeless, or worse, romantic.

Sienna had landed that morning. The flight was uneventful; the taxi was slow. She checked into a small, austere hotel tucked between two narrow buildings in El Born. It wasn't glamorous, and that was why she chose it. She didn't want postcard beauty this time; she needed and wanted clarity.

By noon, she'd walked the length of the city twice. A café he once mentioned, no. A gallery she remembered from a photo he'd posted years ago, no. Nothing, not even the scent of something familiar to him.

By three, she gave up pretending she wasn't searching. And by four, she saw him.

A rooftop bar. He was alone. Reading, of course. Back against the glass railing, hair longer than she remembered, shirt slightly wrinkled. A whisky glass in one hand. Still. Beautiful in that unbearable, unassuming way.

His shoulders filled the chair as though it had been made for him, broad beneath the thin cotton. Even the lazy slope of his posture carried certainty, the kind that made it impossible to look anywhere else.

Her heart clenched. She felt consequences all over her; she should have felt immediate joy. She didn't hesitate. She walked toward him like she had every right to.

He looked up the moment her shadow hit his table.

His eyes caught hers with a steadiness that felt physical, like pressure on her skin. Lined with something older, they didn't just see her; they held her.

"Sienna," he said.

"Hi." She didn't look away.

He gestured to the seat across from him, like he'd been waiting for her. She sat. There was no breathless reunion at that point; they didn't passionately embrace or hug. There was no music swelling in the background. There was Barcelona, heat and her.

"I didn't think you'd come," he said.

"I didn't think I would either."

He studied her face like it was a painting he almost remembered. "So, what now?"

"You left me a letter."

"I know."

"You said I already knew where to find you."

"You did."

A pause.

She let her fingers rest against the condensation on the water glass the waiter had placed in front of her.

"I'm not here for closure," she said finally.

"Good."

"I'm not sure I'm here for you, either."

That made him smile slightly. "Then what are you here for?"

And there it was. The flip.

She'd come to confront him, but he was already turning it back on her.

What do you want, Sienna?

She opened her mouth. Closed it. For once, she didn't have a rehearsed answer.

The sky above Barcelona was a smudged watercolour, burnt gold bleeding into dusky lavender. Somewhere below, music drifted from an open window. Flamenco guitar, slow and aching, paired with the faint rattle of cutlery from nearby balconies. Someone was frying garlic. Someone else was dancing with too much wine in their blood.

The city pulsed with ordinary beauty.

It made Sienna feel out of sync, like she'd stepped into a world where everyone had chosen to live while she was still rehearsing.

The rooftop bar was elevated enough to catch the edge of a sea breeze and the faint perfume of orange blossom from a courtyard she couldn't see. Around them, the early dinner crowd gathered. Locals picking at olives, couples splitting jamón and bravas, tourists marvelling at the view.

But at their table, it was still.

Nico hadn't looked away from her since she sat down.

"You're different," he said, finally.

"You always say that."

"I've never said it like this."

She didn't answer. Her fingertips grazed the rim of her glass like she was trying to remember how to hold something without breaking it.

"I don't want nostalgia," she said.

"Neither do I."

"And I'm not here to pick through the ruins."

"Are we ruins?" he asked.

She looked at him then. Really looked. His eyes were darker than she remembered. Lined with fatigue or time or too many things unsaid. There was a roughness to him now. Honest and not worn down.

"We didn't even get far enough to ruin it," she replied. "We walked away before it had a chance to burn."

He let out a small breath, half laugh, half surrender. "True."

A waiter passed with a tray of small plates: anchovies glistening in oil, fried padrón peppers, crusty bread rubbed with tomato. The smell was dizzying. Sienna hadn't eaten since the airport croissant and was suddenly starving, but hunger felt beside the point.

Nico flagged the waiter. Ordered two vermouths, a plate of Boquerónes, patatas bravas and pa amb tomàquet.

"You remembered," she said softly.

"Of course I did."

The food came quickly, and it was perfect. They ate in fragments, her fingers tearing bread, his fork scraping across the plate. When he leaned forward to reach the plate, the fabric of his shirt pulled across his chest, a reminder of strength that wasn't softened by time.

No conversation. Only the shared intimacy of eating when your body doesn't quite match your mind.

Finally, she said, "Why did you leave the way you did?"

"I thought if I stayed, I'd talk myself out of what I meant."

She met his eyes. "And what did you mean?"

"That it wasn't fair to stay until you figured out whether you wanted the past, or me."

"Is there a difference?"

He leaned forward, voice low and even.

"There is now."

The words landed like a soft, accurate slap. Sienna felt them settle in her chest like they'd always belonged there, waiting for her to hear them properly.

She set her fork down. "You make it sound so clean. Like I had a choice."

"You did."

"No," she said, sharper than she intended. "I had a choice between self-preservation and surrender. And I didn't know how to survive both."

"So, you left."

"I disappeared," she corrected. "I didn't just walk away, I deleted it. You. Us. I convinced myself it had been a summer. A story. A thing I made too big in my head."

Nico leaned back in his chair, his glass poised. "Was it?"

"No," she said, voice low. "It wasn't."

The lights above them flickered on tiny golden bulbs strung between poles, warm against the darkening sky. The rooftop around them brimmed with life, but at their table, time had stalled. She felt like they were inside a snow globe, everything suspended and unreal.

He said nothing for a moment. Then, "I wasn't asking you to stay."

"You didn't have to," she said. "That was the problem."

He tilted his head.

"You were never trying to own me, or fix me, or hold me hostage. You just... saw me. And I didn't know what to do with that."

Her voice wavered on the last sentence, and she hated it, hated that after all these years, her throat could still betray her.

"I didn't need a saviour," she added. "I needed distance. Somewhere to rebuild."

"And did you?" he asked.

"What?"

"Rebuild."

She stared down at the table, at the crumbs scattered across the wood, the smear of tomato on the edge of her plate.

"I built something," she said. "I don't know if it's what I wanted, but I made it strong."

"That's not the same thing."

"I know."

They sat, letting it all hang there. Around them, the air thickened with the scent of grilled seafood and cigar smoke.

Nico finally spoke.

"Do you ever think about what we would've been?"

"Only when I want to punish myself."

He gave a faint smile. "Same."

She looked at him then, and she saw him, not as he had been or as the boy who took photos of strangers in Barcelona, who kissed her on crumbling balconies and whispered stories into her collarbone.

But as the man in front of her now. Still Nico. But not hers.

Maybe never had been.

And still, here he was.

Still waiting.

Still asking.

Not for the past. But for whatever she had left.

She wiped her mouth with the edge of her napkin to stall.

"I thought about reaching out," she said. "So many times."

"But you didn't."

"I always convinced myself it wouldn't change anything."

"Maybe it wouldn't have," he said. "But it would've been real."

That stung.

Sienna sat straighter. "Real doesn't mean better."

"No," he agreed. "But it means you're present. It means you stop letting fear write the second act."

She stared at him. "Do you honestly think I was afraid of you?"

"No," he said. "You were afraid of being known. Of being ordinary. Of letting someone stay when they saw you without the armour."

"And what about you?" she asked, leaning in now. "You speak like you've been on some enlightened path, but you left without looking back. You gave me a letter and no voice. No fight."

"I didn't think you'd want one," he said.

"Bullshit."

Her voice didn't rise, but it sharpened, and the word sliced through the table like silver.

"You gave up as soon as I made it hard. And then you waited for me to do the dramatic thing, hop on a plane, cry in the rain, beg for forgiveness. And when I didn't, you made me the one who ran."

His eyes darkened. "You did run." His shoulders tightened as he said it, the kind of contained tension that suggested he was holding more back than he ever let spill.

"And so did you."

A pause stretched between them; it was tight and furious, full of the years they never dissected.

Finally, he said, "Do you want to keep blaming each other, or do you want to talk like we're not still twenty-two?"

Sienna recoiled slightly, as if the words had a physical weight.

The waiter returned, asking if they wanted another drink. Neither responded. He left.

Sienna looked out over the rooftops, the tile patterns softening in the dusk, everything turning that honey-orange colour only Barcelona seemed to own. The city was indifferent to their drama. Timeless. Watching them spiral with all the patience of a place that had seen lovers unravel before.

"I don't know who you are anymore," she said, barely above a whisper.

"Then ask."

"What do you want?" she said.

He didn't hesitate.

"I want you to stop deciding I'm some myth you once knew. I want you to stop running a highlight reel of who we were and actually look at me. I want you to choose this, now or not at all."

She drew in a long breath.

"You make it sound so simple."

"It's not simple," he said. "It's just honest."

She stared at him. And then, without warning, stood abruptly.

He looked up at her, surprised but not shocked.

"Where are you going?"

She grabbed her bag. "To remember who I am without you in the room."

The door closed behind her with a heavy clunk that felt too final. The staircase was narrow and hot, the kind of heat that stuck to your skin. She didn't wait for the lift. Her heels hit the tile fast, each step a sentence she wasn't ready to say out loud.

Out of the rooftop. Out of that conversation. Out of the version of herself who still, after everything, wanted him to follow.

He didn't. And that made it worse.

On the street, the evening was in full swing. Diners overflowed onto the footpaths. Glasses clinked. Waiters shouted orders through kitchen windows. Two men argued over a football match in Spanish that was too fast for her to translate, and a child pushed a toy stroller across cobblestones like she was on a mission only she knew about.

Barcelona didn't care; it kept going.

She turned left, then right, retracing the streets she'd walked that morning with hope and disorientation. Now she walked with neither. There was a dull ache beneath her ribs and the sense that she had opened something she couldn't close.

She stopped outside a corner bar, the kind with old tile walls and dusty wine bottles lined above the door. It smelled like chorizo and vinegar, and for some reason, it comforted her.

She stepped inside.

The man behind the bar nodded, handed her a glass of Cava before she asked for it, like he'd seen the expression she wore a hundred times before.

She sat on a high stool near the window.

The wine was crisp and zesty. She didn't care.

Her phone buzzed once. She didn't look at it. She already knew it wasn't him.

She hated that part the most, the waiting. Even now. Even after *she* had walked away. Some small traitorous part of her still wanted to be followed. Wanted to be told. *You're not done. We're not done.*

But the door stayed shut. The chair across from her stayed empty.

She took another sip. Then another.

In the reflection of the bar mirror, she didn't look strong. Or fragile. She looked like someone who had come all this way only to meet herself at the centre of it. And maybe that was the point. She'd stormed out looking for distance. What she found was herself, entirely on her own. There was no script or illusion here, a woman in Barcelona, at a bar, drinking alone after telling the one person she'd never stopped loving to go to hell. And meaning it.

Mostly.

The wine was almost gone when she finally looked at her phone. No more messages, just the time. It was late.

She considered going back to the hotel, but the thought of that sterile white duvet and the minibar's sad snacks made her feel ill. Stillness felt impossible. Like surrender.

Instead, she pulled a few euros from her wallet, dropped them on the counter, and stepped back into the night.

The streets had cooled, the stone holding a memory of heat but no longer radiating it. She walked without purpose, without a route. The rhythm of her own feet on cobblestones, the occasional hiss of a scooter, voices rising in bursts from open windows.

She passed a florist locking up, a black cat curled in the doorway. A man in a suit slept sitting up on a bench, head tipped back like he'd surrendered to the day.

When she stopped, she realised she'd circled back to the rooftop bar.

It surprised her. Because her feet had chosen something her head had ruled out. The door was closed now. The lights dimmed. He was gone. And somehow, that helped. It wasn't a romance novel. It was real life.

She sat on the low stone wall across the street, legs stretched in front of her, heels dangling from her fingers. The streetlight above her buzzed, blinking once before settling into a low amber hue. She thought about what she'd said. What *he'd* said.

How easy it had been to go for the jugular when neither of them had protected anything soft for so long. She didn't feel bad about leaving the table, not entirely. But she didn't feel triumphant either. She felt scraped raw. Like honesty always promised to be liberating but never warned you how much it would cost.

She exhaled, pressing her thumb into the sole of her foot. The ache composed her. Somewhere in this city, Nico was walking too.

Maybe alone. Maybe replaying it all in his head the way she was. Maybe not at all. She didn't know. And for the first time, she didn't try to guess.

This wasn't a cliffhanger. This wasn't the end of something tied with a bow. This was the middle, the messy, beating middle where love didn't guarantee you safety, and showing up didn't mean you'd be met. But she'd shown up. And she'd told the truth. Even when it cracked. Even when it didn't fix a damn thing.

She slipped her shoes back on, and turned away from the bar.

She had a room waiting. And maybe tomorrow… a new beginning.

But tonight?

Tonight, she walked away without needing to be followed.

Chapter Seventeen

THE STRANGER

Her new room was smaller but warmer, with fewer mirrors and fewer questions. Room 303 overlooked a courtyard filled with crooked chairs and drying laundry. The tiles outside were cracked and sun-bleached, and a striped towel flapped from a third-floor railing like it had something urgent to say.

Sienna dropped her bag at the foot of the bed and moved into the centre of the room, standing motionless. Her limbs ached not from walking, but from holding too much tension for too long. The fight with Nico had settled somewhere deep in her body, like lactic acid, not pain exactly, more like residue.

She opened the window. The evening air was cool now, threaded with the smell of sea salt, fried garlic, old stone, and late roses. Someone nearby was playing piano badly, but earnestly. She leaned into it.

The room had no robe, no minibar, no selected playlist humming from hidden speakers. It was just a bed, a desk, and a small leather chair with a cracked armrest.

And it was exactly what she needed.

Sienna took off her shoes, pulled her hair loose, and lay on the bed without undressing. For a while, she just stared at the ceiling fan spinning above her. This wasn't heartbreak. This wasn't freedom. This was something else. A reset. The emotional hangover of a woman who had finally told the truth and didn't know what to do with it.

Her phone was silent. No messages from Olivia. No call from Nico.

She didn't know which absence hurt more.

By the time the sun had dipped fully behind the buildings, she was
restless again. Physically restless. She needed to move, to place herself
in the living world, even if just to confirm she still existed inside it.
She changed into black trousers and a soft button-down. She brushed
her hair and applied a bit of lipstick for refinement. Like dressing up
grief in something less obvious.

Downstairs, the hotel bar was nearly empty. A few couples leaned into
each other in corners. A bartender with a sleeve tattoo wiped glasses
with the kind of bored intensity unique to men who thought they were
meant for something more. She took a seat at the bar and ordered a gin
and tonic. The bartender didn't ask her anything and moved like he was
part of the architecture.
She liked that.
She sipped her drink and let the gin melt across her tongue. This was
the first time all day she wasn't performing for herself, for a man, or for
a memory.

She didn't expect company.
Which is why, when the older woman slid onto the stool beside her,
elegant and alone, Sienna didn't brace. She glanced sideways and said
nothing. The woman returned the gesture with a nod and a slight smile,
as if to say: *You're not the only one who needed to come downstairs tonight.*

"You didn't come for the music," the woman said.
Her voice felt practised; it was burnished somewhere between
Marlboro and Moët. Sienna turned slightly, unsure if the comment was
directed at her or into the air.
"I didn't know there was music," she replied.
"There isn't," the woman said, smiling faintly. "Exactly my point."

She had silver hair in a perfect low twist, dark trousers, and a silk blouse that was probably vintage and absolutely intentional. No makeup except a bold lipstick, deep merlot. She looked like a woman who'd been everywhere and had no interest in naming the places.

Sienna didn't want company, but this didn't feel like an intrusion. More like... recognition.

The bartender slid the woman a glass of red wine without asking. Clearly a regular. Or someone impossible to forget.

"Let me guess," the woman said, tilting her glass slightly. "You're either running from something or running toward it. But either way, your shoes hurt."

Sienna smirked. "Close. Only the second part."

The woman arched a brow. "You flew to Barcelona in heels?"

"I flew to Barcelona in fear. The heels were just habit."

That drew a small laugh. "Well. At least you're self-aware."

Sienna sipped her gin. It no longer burned.

"I'm Nora," the woman said, extending a perfectly manicured hand.

"Sienna."

"Of course you are." She said it like a compliment. Or maybe a prediction.

They clinked glasses lightly, without fuss.

"I come here once a year," Nora offered. "Same week. Same room. Same pace."

"Is it an anniversary?" Sienna asked.

"It used to be," she said. "Now it's... proof. That I'm still here."

Sienna said nothing. She didn't have to.

"Love's not supposed to be a riddle," Nora said, as if reading a line from a book they were both halfway through. "But some of us don't learn that until it's already cost too much."

That caught Sienna off guard. Not because it was imposing, but because it wasn't.

She set her glass down slowly. "Was it recent?"

Nora shook her head. "No. But time doesn't dilute truth. It just stops trying to protect you from it."

Sienna glanced down at her hands. Her nails were chipped. She hadn't noticed until now.

"Can I ask you something?" she said.

"You can ask anything. I don't promise answers." Nora replied.

"Do you regret it? Whatever it was?"

Nora smiled again. This one didn't reach her eyes. "Only when I forget who I used to be."

Outside, a Vespa buzzed past the open doors. A waiter dropped a tray and cursed in the alley. Inside, the vibe between the two women softened into something that didn't feel like loneliness.

Sienna leaned back on her stool. She wasn't sure why she hadn't left yet.

Or why she hoped Nora wouldn't.

"Were you in love?" Sienna asked voice low.

Nora didn't look surprised. She took a slow sip of wine and set the glass down with care, like the question had weight.

"Yes," she said. "Utterly. Obsessively. Logically. And badly."

"All four?" Sienna questioned.

"Not at once. That's the real tragedy. You never get them in sync."

Sienna gave a soft, involuntary laugh, the kind you make when something sounds ridiculous and true.

Nora crossed one leg over the other. Her shoes were beautiful: black patent leather, low heel, the kind worn by women who still wanted to be taken seriously but didn't owe anyone height.

"I met him when I was thirty-seven," she said. "Married at thirty-nine. Separated at forty-one. Divorced at forty-four. And I stayed in love with him until fifty-one."

"That's a long goodbye."

"Oh, I didn't say he stayed. I did."

Nora didn't withdraw when she said it. She didn't look ashamed. She was clear.

"Stayed in love with him?"

"No," Nora said. "Stayed shaped by him. That's worse."

The bartender brought another round, unasked for but correct. Sienna wasn't sure whether to thank him or tip him for psychic services.

Nora lifted her glass again.

"I waited years for him to become the version of himself I saw in the first six months. Held the line. Edited myself. Dressed the part. Smiled at his comments. Laughed at the wrong moments. Held the door open for a man who never walked back through it."

Sienna didn't speak. Her throat felt tight.

Nora looked over, her tone softer now. "You're wondering if you're already doing the same."

Sienna didn't answer. She didn't have to.

"Tell me," Nora said gently. "Was he charming? Wounded? Brilliant? All three?"

Sienna gave a small, breathless nod. "He was honest. That's the worst part."

"No," Nora said. "That's the part that leaves the deepest mark."

They didn't say anything for a while. Long enough for the ice in Sienna's glass to melt slightly. The clink of it against the rim felt too loud, like it didn't belong in the space they'd created.

Eventually, Sienna asked, "And once it's there?"

"Now I take myself to Barcelona," Nora said. "Once a year. Stay in a hotel with no expectations. Dress up for no one. Drink alone in bars like this and talk to women who look like they're trying not to repeat history."

Sienna's mouth curled, but not into a smile. Something smaller. Sadder. Something that understood.

"Does it help?" she asked.

Nora looked at her, dead-on.

"It does if you don't lie to yourself while doing it."

Sienna nodded slowly.

The older woman turned back to her drink. "You don't look like a woman who lies to herself. Not anymore."

The room hadn't grown louder, but something had shifted. The clatter of the world outside the bar faded, as if time knew it wasn't welcome right now.

Sienna traced the rim of her glass with her fingertip. She wasn't ready to speak, not quite. But she also couldn't not.

"There was a pregnancy," she said.

The words startled her own ears.

Nora didn't react with surprise, she waited. That was the thing about women like her: they'd already seen the fire and learned how to stand beside it without flinching.

"I didn't tell him," Sienna continued. "I barely admitted it to myself. I was twenty-two, in Barcelona, living in a student hostel with paint-stained sheets and dreams so fragile I was scared to breathe on them." She paused. "And then he happened. Or we happened. And suddenly everything felt... possible. Stupidly, heartbreakingly possible."

"You were scared," Nora said.

"I was in love," Sienna corrected. "Which is the same thing, sometimes."

She laughed, but it caught in her throat.

"I told myself I was protecting him. That I was too young, too unstable, too unprepared to make room for anything more complicated than the two of us already were."

"And were you?"

Sienna looked up. "Yes. But also... no."

"I ended it before I had to make a decision," she said. "When I got home, I pretended it was all just a late period. Or food poisoning. Or stress. But I knew."

"And you left," Nora said gently.

"I left," Sienna repeated.

She didn't realise she was crying until she felt a tear hit her wrist.

"I built a life out of denial. I became successful. I travelled. I bought furniture that matched. But sometimes I'd see a child at an airport, or a father lifting his daughter onto his shoulders, and I'd feel like a thief."

"You weren't a thief," Nora said softly.

"No. But I was a coward."

"No," Nora said again, firm this time. "You were a woman making an impossible choice without a safety net."

Sienna stared at her. "Do you ever stop carrying it?"

"You learn how to hold it differently," Nora said. "Like grief. Or love. It becomes a shape you recognise, even when it stops hurting."

They sat together in that truth, lingering.

Sienna let out a long breath, the kind you only exhale after years of holding something in.

"It's not about getting him back," she said finally.

Nora smiled like she already knew.

"It's about getting you back," she replied.

The glasses were nearly empty now.

Sienna rolled hers between her palms, no longer drinking, but grounding herself. Her body felt warm, but not from the alcohol. From the honesty. From having said what had lived unnamed inside her for so long, like a secret that had finally exhaled.

Nora didn't fill the space. She didn't summarise or soothe. She sat there, perfectly still, the kind of presence that didn't demand attention to command it.

"You always come alone?" Sienna asked.

"Always."

"Don't you get... lonely?"

Nora looked at her with a half-smile. "Of course. But I've been lonelier in company. At least here, I know who's missing."

Sienna knew that kind of loneliness. The type that curled up beside you in a shared bed. The kind you couldn't name in front of friends because everything looked fine from the outside.

"Would you do it differently?" she asked.

Nora paused, her fingers resting lightly on the base of her wine glass. "No," she said. "Because if I did, I wouldn't be the woman sitting here now. And I like her."

It was such a simple statement. Sienna almost envied it.

"Do you think," she began, "it's too late to choose yourself?"

Nora turned toward her fully. "It's only too late when you stop believing your own time is still worth spending."

Sienna let that settle.

The bartender approached with a quiet nod. "Ladies, last round?"

Nora waved him off. "We're done."

He cleared their glasses without a word. The room had emptied, only two tables remained, and even they were already pulling jackets over their shoulders and counting coins in their pockets.

Nora reached for her handbag, then paused. "Thank you for letting me talk. Most women don't listen to other women unless they're looking for themselves in the story."

"I think I did."

"I know you did."

Sienna's limbs felt steadier now. Not light but aligned.

She hesitated. "Will I see you again?"

Nora smiled. "Maybe. But if not, make the choice. Don't let the story keep happening to you."

She leaned in and kissed Sienna once, lightly, on the cheek. Then turned and walked toward the elevator with a graceful finality that said she'd done this before and survived it.

Sienna paused for a long moment.

The bar was full of echoes now, but not the haunting kind. The kind that made room for something new.

She exhaled and picked up her bag, stepping out into the cool night air. The streets hadn't changed.

But she had.

Barcelona was hushed, but not asleep.

The city had that rare midnight stillness, the kind where things aren't dead, they are pausing. A cigarette glowed on a nearby balcony. Somewhere, a mop bucket rolled down a hallway. A woman singing faintly from a terrace above, a sound half-memory, half-dream.

Sienna walked, she didn't have a destination; she had a direction. Forward.

Her heels clicked against the stone, rhythmic, purposeful. She passed the same late-night café she'd noticed earlier, a small place with checked tablecloths and a chalkboard menu that no one had wiped clean in weeks. The scent of grilled peppers drifted out onto the street.

She stopped to notice.

She realised she hadn't really *seen* anything in days. Not properly. Her senses had been hijacked by emotion, by analysis, by the relentless mental gymnastics of trying to read between the lines of every word Nico said or didn't. Now, there were no lines. There was only this. This street and this sudden, almost defiant sense of *presence*.

She made it back to the hotel just before one. The lobby was empty. The night staff gave her a nod, the kind that didn't ask questions. She took the stairs this time.

Her room was cool. Still scented faintly of her earlier perfume and the open window's night breeze.

She undressed, folding her clothes over the chair. She didn't check her phone. For once, she didn't want to know who hadn't messaged.

She climbed into bed, pulled the sheets up, and stared at the ceiling. But it wasn't like the night before. Her body ached in ways that weren't from walking. Her shoulders still carried the rooftop, her back the weight of his eyes. And yet as she slid beneath the sheets, she realised she no longer hated the reminder, she still had skin in this story, and it was hers to feel.

The weight in her chest hadn't disappeared. But it had... rearranged. Shifted into something manageable.
What Nora had said lingered in her mind: *Don't let the story keep happening to you.*
Sienna had let so many chapters write themselves. Or worse, let others hold the pen. She thought about what it would mean to start again, not from the pain, but from the truth. No longer stepping into character or carefully editing, to stop waiting for recognition of who she is as a person, and acceptance of herself.

She saw his face then, not the boy in Barcelona, not even the man across the rooftop table, but the way he'd looked when he said
choose this, now or not at all.
That look still lived in her ribs, but it didn't own them anymore.
She turned off the lamp. The room fell into darkness, but she didn't feel alone in it.
Somewhere down the hall, another guest was laughing. A soft, open laugh that bounced off the walls like music.
Sienna closed her eyes and smiled.
Not because anything was fixed. But because something had begun.
And for the first time in a long time, she wasn't afraid to see where it might lead.

Chapter Eighteen

THE RETURN

The sun rose over Barcelona with a kind of restraint, soft amber stretching across the rooftops, filtering through sheer curtains and making everything look gentler than it was.

Sienna lay still, watching the light crawl up the walls like time whispering. She could still smell salt from the coast if she tried, Barcelona's heat lingering like a secret, the laughter that had spilled out of balconies and nights that never ended. She hadn't thought about the noise, only the feeling of it - that brief summer when everything felt possible. It's already tomorrow.

She hadn't slept much. Not because of the small possibility of her life being in turmoil, it was more like... she was processing. Like her body had needed the stillness while her mind reorganised the files it had kept buried for years. She could still feel Nora's words echoing through her cool, clean cuts of truth that stung less than they clarified.

The hotel slippers were soft, her feet sore from walking the city the night before. Her body still remembered him in fragments, the rough warmth of his forearm against hers in the Spanish heat, the way he moved when he was thinking. It wasn't longing exactly, more a low hum that memory refused to mute.

She padded across the floor, opened the window wider, and let the air in. Barcelona unfolded. And for the first time, she felt herself matching that rhythm. She brewed the in-room coffee - it was terrible - but it smelled familiar and took it out onto the small balcony. Below, a woman in a bright red scarf walked a small dog with more attitude than size. A cyclist weaved between cars. Church bells rang in the distance, measured and rhythmic.

This city had been a pause. A necessary one.

She pulled her robe tighter and sat.

On the table beside her lay her phone. Facedown. As if it could absorb her avoidance. She picked it up and turned it over. No messages. Not that she expected one. She started a new message instead to Nico.

I'm not writing this to ask you for anything.

I just want to tell you what I never did.

That was as far as she'd got. She read it again, exhaled, then deleted the last line.

Too much.

She started over.

I'm going back to New York.

If you want to talk, you know where to find me.

She stared at it. Let it sit. She hovered over send before tapping the back button, then retreated.

Not until she knew this wasn't a reaction. Not until she was clear that this wasn't about hope, it was about closure, or possibility, or maybe finally stepping off the emotional treadmill.

She stretched and turned back into the room. Her suitcase sat open on the bench, half-packed, like even it wasn't sure yet.

The phone buzzed.

Olivia.

"Answer when you're free. Got news. Good news. Call me."

Sienna smiled faintly.

Timing. That damn thing.

Sienna didn't hesitate this time. She hit call.

Olivia picked up on the second ring, out of breath and caffeinated, like she'd been waiting by the phone with a latte and a speech.

"Tell me you're alive," she said.

"Barely," Sienna replied, smiling faintly. "And tragically caffeinated."

"Jesus. I was about to report you missing. Or worse, emotionally hungover."

"That's not inaccurate."

There was a beat, then Olivia softened. "You ok?"

"I had a drink with a stranger who dismantled my entire emotional architecture in under an hour."

"So… Tuesday, then?"

Sienna laughed genuinely, this time. "You'd like her."

"I already do. Now listen, I didn't just call to emotionally rescue you from your latest personal reckoning."

"I'm shocked."

"You should be. Because I come bearing actual, career-altering news."

Sienna sat back down, legs folded beneath her. "Go on."

"The agency, the one from the conference? The one whose rep cried real tears and said you'd changed her life?"

"The same," Sienna replied.

"They want a meeting. In person. Next week."

Sienna felt her pulse shift.

"It's not just one meeting, by the way," Olivia added. "They've asked for a pitch. On you. A vision. What you'd do if you weren't doing what you're doing."

"And they want that from me?"

"They want *you*. The unfiltered, New York-conflicted, wildly brilliant you. I told them you'd be back next week."

Sienna laughed under her breath. "You told them?"

"Don't make me say I believe in you. I've got a reputation to maintain."

Sienna didn't answer right away. She crossed to her suitcase, still half-zipped, and ran a hand over it.

"Are you hesitating?" Olivia asked.

"No. I just… thought I'd feel more conflicted."

"And do you?"

"No. That's the weird part."

Olivia paused. "Then maybe this isn't a return. Maybe it's a reset."

Sienna looked around the room, the soft cream curtains, the black iron railing of the balcony, the narrow mirror that made everything feel taller than it was.

She'd come to Barcelona to run. What she'd done instead was *see*.

Olivia's voice cut back in. "Send me your flight details. I'll have the hotel ready."

"I haven't booked it yet."

"You will."

Sienna ended the call, the phone still warm in her hand. Her fingers drifted back to the unsent message to Nico. She reread it, eyes calm.

I'm coming back to New York.

If you want to talk, you know where to find me.

This time, there was no hesitation.

She hit send.

Then turned to finish packing.

This wasn't about what he would do next.

It was about what she would.

The cab pulled up outside the hotel just after dusk.

New York's heat clung to the windows, the air sticky with midsummer certainty. Sienna stepped out, her hand already pushing her hair off her neck, sunglasses still on even though the light was fading. The city hadn't changed, but she had. And now, it was obvious.

The doorman gave her a polite nod of recognition, but not intrusion.

The lobby doors hissed open, releasing a soft breeze of coated wood, expensive, and something citrusy she'd never been able to name.

She paused before walking in.

She hadn't booked the same room.

She hadn't requested anything, actually.

She asked for a room.

Any room.

The moment she stepped over the threshold, it hit her, a low realisation of awareness. A strange kind of emotional vertigo: *I've been here before, but I'm not the same.*

A woman in a loose summer blazer checked in at the far end of the counter. A couple whispered over martinis in the bar. The elevator chimed somewhere above.

Sienna approached the front desk.

The concierge smiled. "Welcome back, Ms Hartley."

"You remember me?"

He smiled again, eyes crinkling kindly. "You stayed with us before."

Of course. The speech. The crash. The man in the other room.

"Just one key today," she said. "No special requests."

"Of course. We've put you on level seven. Room 709."

She took the keycard without comment and slid it into her bag. She didn't need to ask who was in 710. Or if he was even still here. She wasn't here to find him.

The elevator ride up was smooth, silent, and fast. She didn't look at herself in the mirrored walls; she wasn't avoiding looking at herself at all, it was more the refusal to impress.

Suite 709 was clean and modern. Slightly smaller than the last suite, but it felt… breathable. The windows looked west, onto a brick building with a mural half-faded by the sun. She let her bags fall and, in the centre of the room, listened. No footsteps above or music through the wall. There was a stillness that mirrored her own.

She pulled her phone from her pocket.

Still no reply from Nico.

Not that she expected one.

She didn't reread the message. She didn't pace or unpack immediately. She kicked off her shoes and lay back on the bed fully clothed, arms stretched out wide like she was measuring the space she now took up without apology.

There was something freeing about it. To be and not waiting. Or wondering. The room didn't hold echoes anymore. It held possibilities. And tonight, that was enough.

TSR

She left the hotel just after nine, walking without direction, like the streets themselves might reveal what she hadn't yet articulated.

New York at night was a thrum beneath her feet, trash trucks groaning around corners, streetlights casting fractured halos, steam curling up from manholes like the city exhaling its secrets.

She didn't wear headphones. Didn't need a distraction. Every sound went through her: a busker's guitar, the rhythmic screech of a skateboard, a woman yelling lovingly into her phone. The city wasn't trying to impress her; it existed. And that, somehow, made it feel more honest.

She paused at a crosswalk, waiting for the signal, then crossed before it turned. This wasn't Barcelona, where even a walk felt like an event. This was New York. Keep up or get out of the way. No one was slowing down to see who you were.

She liked the anonymity of it.

She stopped at a late-night bodega on the corner of 58th and Lex and bought a cold bottle of water and a pack of mints, just to do something ordinary. The cashier handed her change without eye contact. Perfect.

Outside, she sat on the bench outside the park entrance, the smaller one nestled between buildings. It was half-hidden, half-forgotten. A place for locals, not tourists.

She unscrewed the water, took a long drink, and let the city stretch. A phrase Nora had said came back to her *Don't build your life on waiting.* Sienna hadn't realised how many of her choices had been made in the name of someone else's momentum. Staying. Hoping. Not texting. Then texting. Not travelling. Then travelling. Always responding. Always orbiting. But now she was her own centre. If he replied, fine. If he didn't, also fine. This wasn't an invitation. It was information.

The bottle sweated in her hand as the breeze picked up. Somewhere behind her, the city carried on, cars sliding past, lights blinking in office buildings where someone was probably finishing a pitch deck or crying over a spreadsheet.

She smiled.

It felt good to belong again. Not to *him*. To *here*.

She tossed the empty bottle in the bin and headed back in the direction of the hotel. This time, her steps had a rhythm; she walked with ease. She walked back into the lobby and pressed the lift button. The doors opened. She stepped inside. Alone.

And this time, it didn't feel like a metaphor.

It felt like movement.

The hallway was dim, washed in golden light, the kind that made everything feel like a movie scene. Her shoes made soft contact with the carpet. She passed suite 710 without looking. Or trying not to look. She wasn't sure which.

Her keycard worked on the first try. Small miracle.

Inside, the suite was still. Turndown service hadn't happened yet. The slightly wrinkled sheets she'd stretched across hours earlier were there, and a faint trace of the perfume she'd put on as an afterthought.

She moved to the window and pushed it open wider. Let the night in.

Then she saw it.

On the console table by the minibar, a cream-coloured envelope sat. Without a hotel logo and no name on the front.

It had a weighty stillness around it.

Sienna stared at it for a moment, unsure whether to feel startled or tired. She hadn't noticed it before. It hadn't been there when she left.

She walked over and picked it up carefully. The flap wasn't sealed; it was tucked with no clues; it seemed like a gesture.

She sat on the edge of the bed and slid the card out.

"You don't owe me anything.
But if you're still curious - Suite 2."

That was it.

She exhaled, tracing the edge of the card like it might reveal more if she touched it differently. But it didn't. It just sat there in her lap, perfectly still.

She looked toward the door. There was no gravity pulling her, nor a sense of hope; she just felt consideration.

He was here.

Had been here.

And he hadn't knocked. Hadn't asked. He'd left a door open, but only if she wanted to walk through it.

This was different.

This wasn't a plea; it was a pivot. A man not trying to be chased, a man offering her space.

She crossed to the bathroom and washed her hands like she was

clearing the static from her body. Looked at herself in the mirror.
Still the same face.
But the expression had changed. She doesn't have to put on an act, she doesn't have to be what everyone else wants her to be, she doesn't have to smile just because it's expected.
She dried her hands. Left the note on the console where she'd found it.
She didn't need to decide now. The suite was hers tonight.
And tomorrow... well, tomorrow had options.

Back on the bed, she pulled the blanket over herself without changing.
Flicked off the lamp. Let the city beat just outside the glass.

Suite 2...710.

So that's where he was. His code for the second room. Or wasn't.
Either way, she wasn't going to knock. Not tonight. But she didn't throw out the card, either.
She placed it inside her book; between pages she hadn't yet read.
Sienna didn't sleep right away. She lay still in the quiet, one hand resting on her stomach, the other open beside her like she'd been reaching for something in her sleep. The note from Nico was folded inside her book on the bedside table, placed like a possibility. The city murmured faintly through the glass. A siren somewhere uptown, the distant clatter of a bin lid closing, a cab engine idling. It was never truly silent here, but tonight the noise felt... irrelevant. The storm was internal now. And she wasn't running from it. She'd sent the message. She'd made the move. And still, she wasn't waiting. That was the shift.

Sienna sat up briefly, turned on the lamp and reached for her water, sipping it slowly, letting the cold settle behind her ribs. The clock on the nightstand glowed
1:17 am.

She didn't know when he'd left the note. Hours ago? Minutes? Had he
passed her in the lift again? Had he watched her walk by the bar?
Or had he simply guessed she'd come back, and that she'd come back
different? It didn't matter.
She set the glass down and turned off the lamp. Darkness wrapped
around her gently, not like an ending, but like a pause. She let herself
stretch out across the sheets, her limbs loose, her breathing calm. The
absence of resolution didn't rattle her this time. There was a strange
peace in not knowing. In not chasing the version of herself that
would've knocked on that door just to soothe uncertainty. She didn't
need to be the woman who had all the answers. She only needed to be
the woman who *stopped abandoning herself to get them.*

Outside, the wind picked up slightly. She turned onto her side and
closed her eyes. Nico existed. Suite 2 existed. The note existed.
But so did she. And for the first time in years, that was enough.

Chapter Nineteen

THE SECOND ROOM

Sienna woke late to sunlight streaming through the curtains. The air was still; the note was still inside her book. She got dressed, wearing a plain black midi dress, sneakers, and her hair pulled back. It was already warm. She told herself it was to get some air. Maybe do some shopping or just wander, but she needed to walk. There was something about Olivia's words that wouldn't stop circling in her head.

What would you do if you weren't doing what you're doing?

She stepped into the hallway and tucked the keycard into the pocket of her jacket. She left the hotel just after eight. The street noise outside made the world feel smaller.

She walked for a while, pausing at a window display that reminded her of Barcelona. A mannequin in a white dress, the sleeves wide and full, like they were meant to dance. She kept walking.

By 10, the sky had shifted. The light over the city was all angles. She hadn't bought anything, although a new outfit might've prepared her for her meeting with the agency; she decided just to be Sienna.

She returned to Deliciae, and the lobby was busier this time. A couple dragging designer luggage bickered gently by the flower arrangement. A child in a velvet blazer twirled in slow, determined circles. The scent of caramel and orange blossom lingered in the air, trying too hard.

She headed to the lift to get ready. She reached into her jacket pocket for her room key.

Empty.

She checked again. The other side. Her bag. Nothing.

Sienna adjusted her sunglasses and walked to the front desk. The concierge looked up, then smiled like he'd been waiting.

"I think I lost my key," she told the concierge, slightly breathless.

She hadn't given her name.

He didn't ask for ID.

"No problem, Ms Hartley. We've already arranged a new one for you."

Before she could question how he knew, he handed her an envelope.

Inside were two keycards, one was hers, the other was not.

710 - Suite 2.

She froze.

"I didn't request," she began.

The concierge smiled. "One more key," he said with a knowing look.

"Sometimes a second room is just that. Other times, it's something else entirely."

"Of course," she said. She kept her expression smooth, but something dropped in her stomach, the unmistakable thud of knowing she wasn't the only one still in it.

She felt the weight of the envelope. Two keys. Two doors. Two versions of the same question.

In the lift, the doors closed automatically, knowing exactly where to take her. She watched the numbers light up 3, 4, 5... Her heartbeat landed somewhere around 6. By 7, she was staring at her reflection.. A woman mid-moment.

Suite 2.

The hallway felt different, darker; there were fewer rooms on this floor.
A small chandelier overhead flickered once and then held steady. The
carpet underfoot felt plush, expensive. It absorbed hesitation.
She turned the corner.
There it was.
Suite 2.

Her hand tightened around the keycard. She hadn't seen Nico. He
hadn't knocked. She wasn't even sure if he was still in the hotel or if
this was a gesture, a coincidence, or something else entirely.
She slid the card into the reader. The light blinked green. The door
clicked.
Her breath caught in her throat, but she pushed it open anyway; she
made a choice to.
The suite smelled faintly of cedar and citrus. Brighter and warmer,
even. But it wasn't the light that hit her; it was the absence.
No shoes by the wall. No luggage. No music.
No, him.
But something was there. On the coffee table, a folded piece of thick
paper, weighted by a key. Not a room key, a real one, silver and cool.
Her shoes silent on the floor, she walked over and picked up the note.

For when you're ready.

That was it.
No "love," or initials. Four words and the possibility of everything.
Her hand curled around the key; she held it.
She was there, in this second room that wasn't his anymore but wasn't
entirely hers either.
She wandered the room, taking in the details because she wanted to
know what this space was *meant* to say.
The walls were a soft, moody grey, textured like an old theatre curtain.

A single abstract painting hung above the bed, brushstrokes wild, crimson and black. The kind of art you either stare at for hours or walk straight past.

On the credenza, a turntable. Modern. Next to it, a small stack of vinyl Nina Simone, Miles Davis, and a Leonard Cohen album that looked almost too fragile to touch.

She ran a hand along the bed's edge. The sheets were still paralysed in its hospital corners. The pillows still sat neatly stacked. The air smelled of fresh linen and some kind of sandalwood candle recently blown out.

This wasn't a man's room. But it wasn't sterile either.

He'd been here. Set this up.

And left.

There was no note about dinner or a time frame. He wasn't holding her with an emotional ransom; he had given her a key.

"For when you're ready."

She turned it over in her hand. It wasn't to another hotel room. It wasn't metaphorical either. This was real hardware. The kind of key that opened a door in the real world. Maybe his apartment. Maybe something else.

You don't owe me anything.
But if you're still curious...

The messages weren't coded. They were deliberate. He'd moved. He's moved rooms and floors. He'd shifted entirely. And he was offering her the same. Nico wasn't chasing her or asking her to follow.

He was showing her what it looked like when someone chose peace over punishment.

She sat down on the armrest of the couch, half-poised. This was the space someone made when they weren't afraid of your answer. He'd given her distance. And a doorway, without obligation or backtracking, not even a second knock. He gave her a pause, held open for her, but not forever. The idea both comforted and unsettled her. She'd spent years around men who needed a reaction to feel real. Nico wasn't baiting her. He was betting she'd figure it out herself. The idea of being trusted to know what she wanted, without manipulation, felt foreign. And electric.

She leaned back slightly and let the thought settle. She didn't need to use the key. Not today or tomorrow. But knowing it existed did something strange to her chest. There was no tightness or ache. More like… *possibility*. The unfamiliar texture of a future not being scripted by someone else.

She exhaled, finally. A long, slow exhale that emptied her chest more than she expected. The room was also hers, for now. The key went into her jacket pocket. She left the suite without really deciding to. It was instinct that too much stillness made her restless, or maybe it was the pressure of sitting inside something meaningful. The room wasn't demanding, but it wasn't passive either. It held energy, expectation, or maybe just readiness.

Outside, the whole floor seemed under-occupied, like she was the only one still orbiting whatever this was. She took the stairs instead of the lift; she needed her feet to meet the ground.

In the street, the city yawned open. It was late afternoon, that golden hour where everything looked more pictorial than it deserved to. People clutched coffee cups like props. Dogs wagged their tails at things only they could see. A couple embraced, soft but loaded.

The key was still in her pocket. She could feel it's cool curve against the fabric of her coat every time she moved.

She wandered, not far, past the bakery where she and Olivia had once devoured almond croissants, past a window of a boutique she couldn't afford when she was younger and could easily afford now but still wouldn't pay those prices on principle.

The world hadn't shifted.

But she had.

She paused at a small bench near a bookstore, half-shaded by a lopsided umbrella. From here, she could see the hotel entrance reflected in the mirrored window across the street. It looked just like it always had. Except it didn't. She pulled out her phone to check the time 5:07 pm. Still daylight. Still her own. No one expected her anywhere. For once, not even herself. She remembered something Nico had said once, years ago, in Barcelona. When they were younger and reckless and thought intimacy was urgency.

"The best kind of tension," he'd told her, "is the kind that doesn't ask to be solved."

Maybe this, whatever they were doing, wasn't a problem to fix. Maybe it was space to hold

Her fingers tightened slightly around the phone. Still no message from him. And still, the key sat against her hip like a heartbeat. She brushed the creases from her jacket and crossed the street without looking twice.

Inside the hotel lobby, the concierge gave a single, knowing nod, as if he knew speaking would ruin something unspoken.

Back in the lift, she hit the button for her floor. She wasn't ready to use the key. But she wasn't leaving it behind either.

She closed the door behind her and let her bag fall with a soft thud to the floor. The room welcomed her, no sharp edges, no demands.

She reached into her pocket; the key was warm. She placed it on the desk like a piece of evidence. Or maybe a mirror.

She didn't mean to sit. Or to linger. But somehow, she was on the armchair by the window, legs curled beneath her, eyes tracing the skyline. The city was beginning to dim. Windows across the way flickered on, one by one. Lives being lived. Lamps glowing. Curtains closing. The choreography of the evening.

She leaned her head against the back of the chair, eyes softening.

And there it was.

A memory. Uninvited. But exact.

Barcelona.

A side street she couldn't name anymore, lit by the yellow blur of hanging lanterns. Nico's hand on her wrist was not possessive, but firm. They were laughing. Then not. Her dress was too thin for the breeze, and she'd said something sharp, too sharp. She remembered the way he looked at her then. Like he was trying to figure out whether she wanted to be understood or just heard.

They'd argued about something stupid. Directions, maybe. A translation. A missed turn. But what stuck wasn't the disagreement; it was the pause after it. The way neither of them walked away. Even then, they'd been practising staying. Even when they didn't know how.

Sienna pulled herself back to the present. Her reflection in the window caught her mid-thought, older, yes, but not brittle. There was something intact about her, even now.

She reached for the key again and held it flat in her palm. It wasn't a symbol. It wasn't a metaphor. It was a door. Real. Hinged and waiting. But it wouldn't wait forever.

Her fingers curled around it, and she felt the cool edge press into her skin. This wasn't about romance. Not anymore. This was about timing. About *readiness*. Maybe he wasn't asking her to pick up where they left off.

Maybe he was asking her to pick up where *she* left off.

To decide not only if she wanted him, but if she wanted to be *in* something. Present. Accountable. Soft, without folding.

Unsure of what she was doing until her feet moved.

She went to the turntable. Flicked it on. Dropped the needle gently on the Cohen album.

Crackle. Pause. Then the rasp of his voice filled the room, low, aching, alive.

Dance me to the end of love.

She didn't dance. But she didn't turn it off either. The song played out and asked nothing in return. When it ended, she let the needle spin in its soft circle. She looked at the key one last time.

Then turned out the light.

O—⚷
TSR

Morning arrived in slats of gold and grey, filtered through curtains she'd forgotten to close. The light slid across the floor, like it was checking if it was welcome.

Sienna blinked awake, confused at first. Then she went still. She was alone.

The key was still on the desk where she'd left it. Its presence didn't press it waited.

She pulled on the robe the hotel provided, padded barefoot to the kitchenette, and made herself a cup of tea. Something warm to hold while her mind recalibrated. Something had shifted overnight.

Not her decision or her timeline. But the *tone.*

She wasn't in suspense. She wasn't spiralling.

She was *here.*

She sat on the edge of the bed, letting her legs dangle like she used to as a kid when the floor felt too far away. The mug warmed both hands.

A knock never came.

There was no text.

No invitation.

Nico had made his move. And now he wasn't making another.

It didn't feel like withdrawal. It felt like trust.

And that was scarier, somehow.

She thought about leaving the suite. About walking the city again. About asking Olivia to meet for a late breakfast and letting herself be distracted by pastry and gossip, and overpriced omelettes. But the thought felt too… *external.*

The world could wait.

For once, she didn't need proof that she existed outside herself.

She'd spent most of her adult life executing decisiveness. Picking the table, the wine, and the hotel. Writing the pitch, solving the problem, managing the crisis. Even when there were moments where she was alone, she'd been choreographing certainty.

Now she was sitting in a room someone had left open for her and doing nothing with it.

And that was the most radical act of all.

She walked to the window; the view was nothing special. Still, it felt… real. Honest. Like she wasn't looking at what she should want, but at what *was.*

The tea cooled. She drank it anyway.

The Cohen album sat still, the needle untouched since last night.

She thought about playing it again.

Instead, she went to the desk, picked up the key, and slipped it into the drawer. She didn't need to decide anything right now. The world would keep spinning. Nico would keep being Nico. And she?

She would stay. At least until checkout.

She pulled on jeans and a T-shirt and grabbed a jacket, brushed her hair with her fingers, and tied it back in a loose knot. She went back to the desk, grabbed the key, and for some reason, she needed to have it with her.

She opened the door and stepped into the hallway. Stepping forward, she was not going to search or flee this time.

The hallway hushed in that late-morning lull where guests were either sleeping in or already gone. Sienna walked toward the lift, her pace measured. She had no plan, no destination. Just a sense that she needed air, answers or both. But before she reached the end of the corridor, she heard it. The soft sound of footsteps, certain, and familiar.
She turned instinctively.
Nico.
He rounded the corner like he wasn't expecting anyone, like he belonged there, which he did. His eyes lifted, caught hers, and for a moment neither of them moved.
Then he stopped.
A beat.
Another.
And then, softly, "Took a wrong turn?"
She exhaled a breath she didn't realise she'd been holding. "No. Right one."
A flicker passed between them, history, maybe or recognition of who they were now, instead of who they'd been.
He nodded once. "You found the key."
"I did."
He didn't reach for her or step closer. But his gaze stayed fixed, as if her presence in the hallway told him more than words could. They both stood motionless. The hallway felt tighter than it should have. Airless.
Sienna held her ground.
Nico's eyes were locked on hers. No trace of surprise. He'd been expecting this or hoping. His expression gave nothing away, except maybe the faint tension in his jaw. She didn't look away. She couldn't.

He stepped forward, just the weight of something real. He was barefoot. A dark shirt. Damp hair curled slightly at the back of his neck. She felt every detail like static against her skin.

He stayed right where he was, close enough to feel him, but not close enough to do anything reckless. The light overhead buzzed faintly. Somewhere down the corridor, a door clicked shut. Neither of them registered.

"I left it for you," he said.

"I know."

"You went in."

She gave the smallest nod. "You weren't there."

"I didn't want to be."

That burned. She wasn't sure why. He caught the flicker of it in her face and added, "It wasn't a test."

Sienna shifted her weight but didn't back off. "Then what was it?"

"A start."

He didn't say more. He didn't need to. She reached into her jacket and pulled the key from her pocket. Held it between two fingers.

"This isn't subtle," she said.

"No."

"Is this how you do it now? Invitations without instructions?"

He looked down for a moment, then back at her. "I didn't want to write the ending this time."

Her fingers curled around the key.

"I don't know what I want," she said.

"I'm not asking for a decision."

"But you're still standing here."

"I am."

Another beat.

Then she stepped forward. Closer, almost into his arms. Close enough to smell that faint smell that had become synonymous with him, that made her want him. Close enough to remember exactly how it felt to stand in the eye of a storm and not be afraid.

He didn't touch her, and she didn't ask him to. But something passed between them: *understanding, invitation, restraint, electricity.*

They stood like that for another breath. Then she took another step forward. But the space between them changed.

"I should go," she said, voice lower now.

"You don't have to."

"I know."

She studied him, taking in every detail. Then turned slightly, as if to leave. A half-step, enough to feel the distance. She didn't take another. He didn't stop her. But something anchored her. The key in her hand. The heat in his gaze. The gravity of standing still when you could run. She turned back.

She could have said a dramatic line or proposed a resolution, a shared stillness that felt like the start of something dangerous and beautiful lingered instead. She walked toward the second room and stepped inside; she left the door open. He let the door ease shut behind them.

Chapter Twenty

THE STAY

Sienna positioned herself in the middle of the room; the same stillness from the corridor, only now it was sealed inside and powerful.

Nico waited a few feet behind her; she felt him before she turned. Heat at her back. The hum of a presence she knew in the body first and in the mind a breath later.

She faced him. She could feel it. The quiet in his eyes never felt passive; it felt like restraint. He took her in slowly, the way a photographer judges light, and the attention landed on her skin like a touch.

"You followed me," she said, steady.

"I didn't want the hallway to be the last thing," he answered.

Her breath hadn't quite landed where it should. It hovered, caught somewhere too high in her chest.

"You left a key," she said.

"For later," he replied. "For a life for us where the walls aren't temporary." He wasn't promising forever; he wanted her to know he wasn't clocking out. Her mouth lifted at one corner. That word. Us.

"And if I hadn't taken the key?"

"I'd have checked out. Got on a plane. Gone somewhere, I didn't have to think about you every five minutes."

"Maybe we don't need a plan," he said. "Maybe we just need to stay."

She stepped closer. "I'm here," she said, quieter now.

"I know."

"Show me you do."

He closed the last of the distance, careful and sure, and waited that fraction of a second that used to undo her.

She lifted her face and met him. The first kiss was simple, mouth to mouth. A pause for breath. Another.

Heat gathered at once and then in waves. His hand found the back of her neck. Her fingers slid under the open collar and learned the temperature of him.

She tasted last night's questions burning off. She let them.

When they parted, he stayed close.

"You feel the same," he murmured.

The room steadied around them. She took his wrist and led him to the window. City light laid itself across the floor in a pale rectangle. Their shadows crossed and became one, then separated, then met again as they turned. Her reflection hovered in the glass. Behind it, his.

The light caught the rich texture of his hair, dark, thick, salt and pepper throughout that seemed too artlessly perfect, as though he hadn't spent a moment on it. When he turned, it wasn't the chiseled jaw that demanded attention, but the way his eyes found hers. They were a startling, clear blue, the kind you'd see on a summer sea. But in his left iris, a small, stubborn fleck of brown stood out, a beautiful imperfection that made him seem more real, less a statue and more a person. His shoulders, broad enough to fill the entire frame of the window, spoke of a kind of formidable strength, yet the gesture with which he ran a hand through his hair was almost boyish.

The corners of his mouth turned upward in a slight, apologetic smile when he ever realised Sienna was watching him. It was a small motion, and for a moment, it completely softened the stern angles of his face, the high cheekbones, and the dominant brow. It was a kindness that was like a simple, deep-seated reflex.

He seemed to carry the weight of a thousand thoughts behind those sea-blue eyes, as if the world was a book he was constantly trying to read, and each person in it was a chapter he was determined to understand. His hands were large, with fingers that looked capable and strong, yet he was using them now with a surprising delicacy. He was a paradox of a man: a fortress of a physique with an unmistakable streak of gentleness, an overwhelming presence who held himself with a quiet humility.

"Look," he said, eyes on her rather than the view, "I don't have a speech, but I can tell you what I want."
"Say it." She asked.
"I want the ordinary and the wild. Coffee and honesty. A body I know because I stayed long enough to learn it."
Her breath caught where it mattered. "Then learn."
He kissed her again, deeper now, and she opened to it. His hands travelled with patience and intention. Shoulder. Spine. Waist. She answered with the same.
Stubble grazed her cheek, and she liked the small sting of it. He moved more slowly than he had any right to, and in that careful, intimate contradiction of Nico, she could feel herself starting to fall deeper.

"I hate that you can still make me feel like this," she whispered.
Sienna turned, her eyes dragging across the lines of his face like she was memorising something she already knew too well.

He leaned forward, "I didn't leave that key to play games Sienna, I left it because I didn't want to lose *you* without trying."

Something cracked. Almost open enough to let light through.

"I didn't think you would stay for me," she murmured.

He exhaled. "It's always been us."

"I'm tired of missing you."

The air had finally exhaled with her. It was a relief. She walked to the bedroom door. Opened it. Paused in the frame.

She turned to him. "Are you coming?"

He crossed the room and followed. No promises or games right now, only the choices they made, again. The bedroom had been waiting. Like it already knew what would happen here and was holding its breath.

Nico closed the door behind them, softly. He waited there, watching, like he was afraid she might disappear again. Sienna walked to the edge of the bed and sat down. The mattress dipped under her, plush and impossibly soft, but she barely noticed.

"Tell me." She said.

He moved more slowly, as if his body was still catching up to the moment. He sat beside her, close enough for her skin to register the nearness.

"I thought about Barcelona every day," he said. "Because I didn't get to *know* you. Not really. I had your laugh, your lips, your scent, and then you were gone."

"You had more than that," she said.

"I didn't know what would happen." He turned to face her. "I couldn't predict the future and know you would get pregnant, Sienna."

The words sat heavily between them.

"I tried to find you. And I figured if you wanted to be found, you would've left a clue."

She stared at her hands. "I didn't even know how to leave the country properly, let alone a clue."

"I know that now."

She finally looked at him. "It was a boy."

He looked away for a second, as if bracing against the weight of her words. The air shifted. For a second, neither of them could remember how to breathe.

"I'm sorry," he said.

"I know."

The room held the weight. Neither of them tried to change it with pretty lies. He reached out then and brushed a strand of hair from her cheek.

"I never wanted you to carry that alone," he said. "I wanted you before, and I still want you now."

She studied him, as if she could measure truth in eyelashes and breath.

"Say it again," she said.

"I want you now."

Her hand found his, "I don't know how to do this," she admitted.

"Then we'll figure it out badly."

She laughed, too tired to fight the softness. "I have rules."

"I expect nothing less."

"No secrets. No disappearing. No rewrites."

"Agreed."

"And no falling asleep mid-sex."

His smile cracked wide. "Now that one I *cannot* promise."

She pulled him down by the collar and kissed him slowly, deeply, like she was tasting all the years between them. It was so certain, so real. And this time, when the sheets tangled, the room warmed, and the glasses on the nightstand sat untouched, they both stayed.

The next morning arrived like a whisper. There was light, creeping in through sheer curtains and landing gently on their bare shoulders. Sienna woke, registering warmth before memory. Nico was beside her, still asleep, one arm slung across her waist like it belonged there. She stared at the ceiling, letting it all sink in. She wasn't dreaming, or having a flashback, or some glamorous regret this time. He was real. Here. Again for her. His breathing was slow, even. She studied the faint lines around his mouth, the shadows beneath his eyes, the silver at his temples that hadn't been there years ago. He looked better. Broken in. She brushed a finger along his chest, light enough not to wake him. His skin twitched anyway.

"I know you're awake," she murmured.

"You talk in your sleep," he mumbled.

She raised a brow. "Do I?"

"You kept saying, 'Don't miss your cue.'"

She groaned, burying her face into his shoulder. "I hate that that's probably true."

He laughed softly, the kind of sound that made the room feel more alive. He wrapped both arms around her now, pulling her closer without asking.

"You stayed," she said into his skin.

"I did, and so did you."

"I was half-expecting a note and a disappearing act."

"Not our style anymore."

She pulled back just enough to see his eyes. "So, what *is* our style now?"

"Lingering. Apologising. Earning things properly."

She ran her hand through his hair. "That sounds exhausting."

"I'll make coffee."

They lay there a few more minutes, neither of them in a rush to ruin it with clothing or conversation. Eventually, Sienna slipped out of bed, wrapping herself in the thick grey robe hanging behind the door. She padded into the suite's kitchenette while Nico rummaged through drawers like a man on a mission.

"Why are the mugs always at knee level in hotels?" he asked.

"So, you have to bend over. It's a service to the person behind you."

He grinned. "You're welcome, then."

Sienna leaned against the counter. "What do we do now?"

He handed her a coffee, his expression softening. "We don't rush it."

Nico stepped in closer. "We do what we didn't do before. We talk. We show up. And when we get scared, we *stay* scared, together."

She stared at him, her throat suddenly tight. "You say that like you mean it."

"I say that because I do." And somehow, in that instant, it stopped being a hotel suite and started feeling like something else. A beginning. She took a sip of coffee, closed her eyes, and smiled. This time, she wasn't falling. She was choosing.

They took their time getting dressed, the way people do when they know the clock won't win and all they want to do is stay. Sienna ran a hand through her hair in the mirror, catching Nico's reflection behind her. He was watching her like she was a story he hadn't finished reading. She didn't mind it. Not this time. She smiled; she had forgotten how much her face used to ache around him from smiling too much. Their bags had not been opened, there was no rush to check out, and no plan scribbled in a notebook. Only today. And maybe tonight. He came up behind her and placed his hands on her waist.

"I was thinking," he said.

"Oh god."

He ignored that. "We could leave the hotel. Go outside. See what the rest of the city looks like when we're not hiding."

She gave him a look. "You mean, like normal people?"

"I mean, I want to see you walk beside me. In daylight."

She paused, then turned to face him, a small smile tugging at her mouth. "We're not a movie, you know."

"No," he said, pressing a kiss just beneath her jaw. "We're just a very expensive documentary."

She giggled and let herself lean into him, her voice low. "Just promise me you won't get all sentimental on me in public."

He kissed her properly then, deep and slow and sure. "No promises. But I'll try."

TSR

They stepped out of Suite 2 just after midday. The hotel hallway looked the same, but something about it felt different. Sienna paused as they reached the lift.

"You ever think about what would've happened if we'd stayed in Barcelona?" she asked.

"All the time," he said. "But then I remind myself we weren't ready."

"Are we ready now?" Sienna asked.

He took her hand, "Now we are."

At the lobby, Olivia was waiting, pretending to read a magazine she clearly wasn't interested in. Her eyes widened the second she saw them. Sienna braced herself. But Olivia just gave her a small, knowing nod. Approval, with an eyebrow raise. It was the most restrained *I told you so,* she had ever seen. Outside, the sky was overcast. The city stretched in all directions. They stepped into it together. This was a possibility. One worth staying for.

The kind that lasted *if you let it.*

Chapter Twenty - One

THE CHOICE

Sienna watched the light move across the carpet and climb the edge of the duvet. She followed it all the way to Nico.

Is this what normal felt like?

This - the possibility of something lasting, that would only become real if she was willing to nurture it instead of forcing it into shape.

Nico smiled into the pillow. "Hi."

"Hi." She heard her own voice and almost didn't recognise its softness.

He rolled onto his side. "Breakfast in bed or reckless street pastry?"

She considered. "Reckless street pastry that we pretend is a well-balanced meal, no, actually let's do breakfast in bed."

"Ahh, I knew it - a woman after my own heart."

He leaned over and kissed her on the cheek, then grabbed the room service menu.

They sat together cross-legged on the bed like two new people. The past was past, and whatever new connection they had was a fresh start, not a rehash of what was.

Sienna watched Nico scroll through the hotel's breakfast menu, his stomach gurgling.

"You know that if you are really hungry, you can order whatever you like, *and* as much as you like, right?" she teased, tying her hair into a loose knot.

"I'm comparing omelette descriptions. There's an art to it on this menu," he said.

They were doing it again. The easy back-and-forth. The illusion of something settled. He looked up at her; they grinned at each other like thieves. It felt easy. It felt dangerous.

After breakfast, they ventured out into the city, through the streets she'd grown up memorising, the rhythm of traffic, the smell of bagels and rain-soaked concrete, all of it both foreign and familiar now that she was seeing it with him. It was the kind of morning that didn't demand plans, only movement. The summer air was warm, full of car exhaust fumes, coffee, and a mix of street food like roasting nuts and pizza combined with that faint, metallic city pulse that made everything feel possible.

They wandered aimlessly until a small independent bookstore appeared, wedged between a florist and a café that already had a queue of people pretending not to stare at each other. Inside, the air was cool and heavy with paper, dust, and memories; it was calm and safe. Nico trailed a finger along the shelves like he was reading them by touch. He found a dog-eared photography annual and made a small, pleased sound that landed somewhere directly behind Sienna's ribs. She watched him for a moment - the way he bent slightly to read the fine print, how absorbed he became when the world narrowed to something he loved.

She drifted to another aisle and pulled a design journal she didn't need, but when she turned back, he was holding a thin paperback - *The Little Prince*. He studied the cover, then looked at her. "It reminds me of you."

She smirked. "What are you trying to say?"

She took it from him, brushing his fingers by accident.

"It's the kind of book that tells you everything you already know but pretend to forget."

He smiled, that quiet, knowing kind. "Then it belongs with you."

She knew what he was implying, but she bought it anyway.

When they left, the sunlight was sharper, the air brighter. They walked close enough for their shadows to brush and separate. By the time they reached the park, the city had slowed again. They shared an iced coffee, which Nico insisted he hated, with pigeons negotiating airspace around their feet. They talked about nothing for a while - album covers, a dog that kept choosing the wrong owner - until the quiet stretched and stayed. Sienna looked over at Nico, the light catching the flecks in his eyes. He caught her gaze and smiled, a soft, genuine expression that reached all the way to her bones. It would've been perfect if it didn't feel like the calm before a storm, but his smile didn't quite hold.

A flicker of something shadowed his eyes, gone almost before it appeared, and his fingers tightened around his cup for a fraction of a second. The easy quiet lingered, but it had changed. The air felt heavier, thicker with the things they weren't saying. The perfect, effortless afternoon had been stripped away, leaving behind a chill she couldn't ignore. She finally broke the silence, the words feeling fragile in the stillness.

"This feels easy," she said, watching the ice slide in his cup.

He didn't look up. "It is."

She traced the sweating side of the cup with her thumb. The cold seeped into her skin.

"That's the part that scares me," she admitted softly.

"I know," he replied, his voice barely a whisper.

"But?"

His fingers tightened on the cup; he didn't say anything. He didn't have to. They both knew this day didn't exist outside this bubble. At some point, someone had to go. Someone had to choose.

Two hours later, Sienna met Olivia at a café off West 12th. The place was aggressively rustic; plants in old teapots, waiters who looked like unpaid poets and a menu that featured an overwrought poem beside the daily special, a 'Deconstructed Toast' for an exorbitant price.

Olivia arrived in head-to-toe black, sunglasses on indoors like she was famous or hungover, or both, holding an iced chai.

"You look suspiciously fresh and hydrated," she said, sliding into the booth. "Did someone finally get laid properly? I'm inferring high-quality activities."

Sienna rolled her eyes. "Hi to you too."

Olivia leaned in. "Spare me. Did you sleep? Like, *sleep* sleep? So, is he staying? Are you staying? Or are we staging an intervention at JFK?"

Sienna sipped, deadpan. "There was horizontal activity, and I don't know yet."

Olivia narrowed her eyes. "That's a lie. You *do* know. You just don't want to say it out loud in case it makes it real."

Sienna took a long sip of her drink.

Olivia grinned. "There it is. The 'I've caught feelings, but I'd rather file it away and pretend it's not happening than admit it' face."

"You're not helping."

"I'm not trying to help. I'm trying to provoke. Different sport."

Sienna laughed, even though she didn't mean to.

Olivia tapped her straw against the glass. "Here's my thesis. You've spent years being the woman who leaves before someone else gets to. That's power, until it's not. If he's who I think he is?

"Look," Olivia said, softer now. "You can't sleep next to someone and pretend it's just comfort. That man makes you sit up straighter. Don't confuse that with tension. That's called *being alive*."

Sienna stared into her glass.

"Just… don't let comfort win," Olivia added. "It's a terrible ending."

Olivia stirred her drink. "Can I just say," she began, "for someone who finally got her happy ending or at least the deluxe king-size version of it, you're being very *meh* about this."

Sienna gave her a look. "I didn't say I was *meh*."

"You're *emitting* meh. It's in your body language. I'm fluent."

She folded her arms. "It's not that simple."

"It *never* is. But sometimes it is."

"Very helpful."

Olivia leaned across the table, lowering her voice like a gossip but with the intensity of a surgeon about to call time of death.

"You're scared. I get that. You've been carrying your independence around like a designer handbag for years, and now someone's asking if they can hold it for a minute, and you're clutching it like it's got diamonds and state secrets inside."

Sienna stared at the table.

"I'm sorry, do you want me to lie?" Olivia asked. "Say it's fine to not know? That maybe this is just a phase? That you should 'follow your heart'?" She made air quotes so sharp they could cut glass.

"I was hoping for something a little more… supportive."

"Oh, honey," Olivia said, sitting back, "this *is* supportive. You've got a man who flew halfway across the world, tracked you down like a character in a French film, and instead of love-bombing you or pulling some Nicholas Sparks shit, he *waited*. He let you come to him."

Olivia pointed her spoon at her. "You know what that is? That's grown-up love. That's love with no ego. That's the love women write monologues about on staircases in TV finales."

"Wow," Sienna muttered. "You've really been saving that one up, haven't you?"

"Damn right I have." Olivia dropped the spoon with a satisfying clink. "Look, I'm not saying he's perfect. No one is. But I've known you for over a decade, and I have *never* seen you look at anyone like this. Not even that Swedish architect you almost moved to Stockholm for."

"Don't bring up Erik."

"I *will* bring up Erik. Erik cried when he spilled kombucha. This man? He looks at you like he wants this to last."

Sienna exhaled hard through her nose.

"I just don't know if I can *trust* it," she said. "This version of us. It feels like a story. And stories don't last."

Olivia softened. "Then maybe it's time you stop writing the ending before you've lived the middle."

Sienna looked down at her hands. Her fingers curled in like they were trying to hold something invisible.

"Ask yourself one thing," Olivia added. "Do you want him gone? Or are you just scared he might actually *stay*?"

Sienna stared at a crack in the table like it might offer help, she didn't answer. She didn't need to. The look on her face gave everything away.

"Try wanting without drafting the exit plan in the same breath."

They sat with that. Then Olivia smiled, wicked again. "Also, your skin looks unreal. Whatever happened last night, continue."

Coffee finished, questions unanswered, they walked back to the hotel, arms linked. Neither said much. Some decisions ask for nothing first. They had barely taken three steps down the hallway before the elevator dinged and opened. A man stepped out holding a takeaway coffee tray, a paper bag, casual as hell in jeans and a black T-shirt, hair slightly mussed, looking like the kind of man you kick yourself for *not* sleeping with and also the kind you hate yourself for letting stay for breakfast – Nico. He slowed when he saw Sienna. His eyes flicked to Olivia, then back to Sienna, checking for cues.

"This is my friend," Sienna said, light but sure. "Olivia."

He offered Olivia a small, respectful nod. "Hi Olivia, nice to meet you."

"You must be Nico," Olivia replied.

His smile was polite, cautious. "Guilty."

She didn't offer her hand. Just looked him up and down, like she was assessing damage.

"You don't look like a problem," she said.

"Most problems don't. At first." He replied.

Sienna elbowed Olivia in the ribs.

Nico's smile faded slightly. "Are you always this direct?"

"I'm usually worse."

He looked at Olivia for a long second, his smile turning real.

"She's lucky to have you."

"She *is*," Olivia said. "I like you, so far. So, no pressure."

His brow lifted slightly, amused but not dismissive. "Noted."

He understood it. He smiled briefly, then turned to Sienna.

"Room?" he asked.

"Five minutes," she said.

He glanced back and then walked down the hall.

Sienna slapped Olivia on the arm, "Olivia, OMG!!"

Olivia bumped Sienna's shoulder. "Well, you know I don't miss opportunities. He looks at you like he can exhale."

"I hate how much I like that."

"Good. Hate it. Means it's worth the risk, ciao for now."

Sienna returned to the second room. The city felt heavier than usual. Maybe it was the humidity, or maybe it was what Olivia had said echoing in her head like a bell that wouldn't stop ringing.

Nico was on the couch, his legs stretched out, bare feet crossed at the ankle. He was flipping through a hardcover book they'd picked up that morning, but he wasn't really reading. She knew the difference now, the subtle pause when he turned a page, the way his hand hovered over the corner too long. He was pretending to be calm.

"So, I finally met Olivia", he said, glancing up.

"You did", she replied, placing her bag gently on the armchair.

Sienna poured a glass of water. She didn't sit down or take off her shoes. The air between them was thick with something unspoken.

Nico set the book down. "I have a flight tomorrow. Morning."

She turned to him. "You booked it?"

"Yeah."

"Back to Spain?"

"Barcelona," he said. "For now."

The final words hung there.

"I thought you said you didn't want to leave," she said, gripping the edge of the benchtop.

"I don't," he said. "But I also don't want to keep showing up in a version of your life where I'm not permanently *in* it."

Her throat tightened. "You *are* in it."

"I'm in a hotel room," he said gently. "I'm in between. That's not the same."

He crossed to her intentionally, slow but sure.

"I meant it, Sienna. I'd stay. I *will* stay. But not if it means you're waiting for something to go wrong, so you don't have to feel guilty when I leave."

She opened her mouth to speak, but he held up a hand to finish.

"I'm not here to be chased. But I've come as far as I can without you meeting me halfway."

She looked at him, her whole body tight with resistance. "So, what if I don't make some sweeping declaration? That's it?"

"No," he said. "If you don't *choose* it, that's it."

He paused, then added, "I'll be downstairs at eight. The hotel bar. I've booked a corner table. No keycard. No suite number. No tricks. Just a place and time. And a choice. If you come," he said, "I'll know you're ready. If not, then I'll leave. There will be no hard feelings, only honesty."

He stepped close enough to kiss her but didn't. He pressed his mouth to her forehead instead, a touch that felt like both blessing and boundary.

"I'm not challenging you Sienna," he said. "I'm trusting you."

He left with his bag, the door closing with a soft click behind him.

Sienna stared at nothing; the suite still smelled like him.

And for the first time in days, she had no idea what to do next.

She lingered for a long time after the door shut.

She felt hollow, like someone had pulled the stuffing out of her and left the shell standing. The room got very loud and very quiet at the same time. She glanced at the spot where his shoes usually sat. Gone.

The book he'd been reading, *The Little Prince*, ironically was closed... sitting on the table like it had been dismissed. She picked it up and flipped through it. She didn't see dog-eared pages or underlines. She saw clean, untouched sentences about foxes and love and leaving. Sienna sat down, finally, because her legs didn't want to hold her anymore. He hadn't yelled. Hadn't begged. He'd given her *every* out. The kind that hurt more than any blow-up or breakup line ever could. Because he hadn't made her feel cornered. He'd made her feel seen. And somehow, that was worse.

She looked around the room, it was the same as it was before, back when she thought it was romantic, this game of cat and mouse across hotel floors and shared lounges. Now it looked like a clock ticking. She thought about what Olivia had said. About not writing the ending before living the middle. About whether she wanted Nico gone or was just afraid he might actually stay. And the truth was…She didn't know how to do *real*. Not with him. Not after everything. Not when it meant giving up the version of herself she'd spent years curating. Professional. Composed. Untouched by past wounds. Letting him stay meant taking her hands off the wheel. She hated the surrender of it, the risk of wanting something she couldn't control. But she also wanted the quiet it promised.

The steadiness. The chance to stop fighting gravity for once.

At 7:04 p.m., she was still sitting in the same spot.
And in less than an hour, she'd either walk into that bar and change everything, or she'd sit here, in a room built on almosts, and let him walk away.
Again.

Her suite's bathroom mirror had terrible lighting. Not the soft, flattering kind you get in films, but the harsh, overhead kind that showed every uneven patch of skin and every line the last few years had left behind. Sienna stared at her reflection anyway. She was still wearing the same clothes from earlier. Safe. Neutral. The kind of outfit you could cry in or leave in. The kind that didn't take sides.

The hotel clock read 7:26 p.m.
She opened the closet, pulled out her suitcase, and unzipped it slowly. The dress was still there. Satin. Deep forest green. A little dramatic. A little reckless. She'd packed it, thinking she'd never wear it. She told herself it was for an awards night that didn't exist or a dinner she wasn't attending. But she knew the truth. It was *that* dress. The one from Barcelona. Not the exact one. She'd long since donated that in some act of forced detachment, but this one was close enough to haunt her. Same cut. Same slinky defiance. Back then, she'd worn it to seduce him. Now, it felt like she was wearing it to see if he still meant it.
She held it up to herself, staring at her reflection. And for once, she didn't see the twenty-something version of herself she kept trying to forget. She saw the woman she'd become. Less forgiving. More deliberate. Still scared but no longer ruled by it. She slid the dress over her head. The fabric kissed her skin like it remembered her. A touch of mascara, a flick of a cat's eyeliner, a nude blush shade lipstick. She wasn't dressing up to be adored. She was dressing like a woman who

knew she was wanted and finally believed it.

At 7:42, she slipped on her heels.

At 7:45, she stood at the door, hand on the knob.

No one was telling her what to do. Not Olivia, not Nico, not the remnants of every man who'd left her before he could be left. She owed herself an ending that wasn't written in retreat. One that didn't involve locking the door and hiding under the covers until it all passed. Then she did something she hadn't done in a long time.

She smiled at her reflection. Not because she looked perfect, but because for the first time in a very long time, she looked *ready*. Her fingers curled around the handle. She let out a breath. And opened the door. Sienna stepped outside the suite.

She wasn't nervous. She was… rehearsing. At least, that's what she told herself. Say something casual. Say something real. Say anything *except* "I didn't know if you'd be here," because that would be tragic.

Just then, the lift behind her pinged open. "Big night?" a voice said. She turned slightly. A young woman in a hotel uniform stood nearby, holding a stack of champagne flutes. Sienna nodded, too poised to ask *what gave it away*.

The staffer gave a sympathetic smile. "Don't worry. You look incredible. And if it's a proposal, I'm here for it. We had one last week. He cried before he even got the ring out."

"It's not a proposal," Sienna replied.

"Even better," she said. "Those ones always end with kissing in the elevator." Sienna smiled. Just slightly.

"Good luck," the woman added, slipping through a side door.

The hallway fell silent again. Sienna waited for the next lift. One breath in. One second to decide.

And then she got in and went down to the bar.

The bar was dimly lit, intimate in that refined hotel way, low lamps, soft jazz from nowhere, tables spaced out like secrets.

Nico was standing at the far end of the bar, facing the window. Dark shirt, sleeves rolled, a whisky glass in his hand. He didn't turn immediately.

He felt her first. She knew he did; she saw it in the way his shoulders eased, then squared. It was recognition. Like her presence had landed before her voice did. Then he turned slowly. And smiled. She stepped forward with certainty in her heels on the floor.

"You came," he said. He slid his hands in his pockets, then out again, nervous for him.

"I almost didn't," she replied.

"Why did you?"

She stopped a few feet in front of him. "Because I finally got tired of leaving before things get good." His eyes searched her face like there might be small print, searching for doubt. "What now?"

"Now," she said, voice steady, "I'm asking you not to leave."

He set the glass down. "Then say it."

"Stay." She said.

That one word cracked the space between them wide open. He crossed it and kissed her. Without hesitation, heat and history and something entirely new. Her fingers found the line of his jaw. His found her waist. The kiss deepened, it held steadiness and the kind of ache that stands up straight, but there was no rush like they finally had time.

When they pulled apart, breathless, her forehead rested against his.

"I didn't bring a plan," she whispered.

"Good," he said. "You won't need one."

She laughed. Then kissed him again, and the world unspooled without telling them what to do next.

And this time, when they held each other

They stayed.

Chapter Twenty-Two

AFTERSHOCK

The world came back in fragments. The faint buzz of the minibar, the rhythm of city traffic seven floors down, the warmth of someone still breathing next to her. Sienna opened her eyes to sunlight filtering through the curtains, a thin line across the sheets that looked almost deliberate, as if it were choosing what to reveal.

Nico was half awake, one arm tucked under his head, the other resting near her hip. He looked effortless, the kind you only get when someone's actually slept beside you, not just spent the night. She stayed like that for a while. Watching. Studying the way his chest rose and fell. The silence between them felt charged, as if sound might break the spell. For a second, she just stared at the ceiling, her brain sprinting in every direction at once.

Holy shit. He's here. I'm here. We're doing this. What now?

Her life was not waking up next to someone who looked like a European fever dream.

Did they check out together? Buy milk? Merge calendars?

She stared at him. Her mind started doing what it always did, cataloguing the impossible:

Would he go back to Barcelona, pack up his life, and move here? Would he go back and decide he wanted to stay there, rather than being with her?

Does he even like New York? Will his toothbrush live next to mine?

Does he own furniture?

Do I need to shave my legs again or is this a long-term thing?

It hit her: she didn't have a plan for this. Not even a rough draft, and honestly, part of her didn't want to talk about what came next. Not because she didn't care, but because she did. Too much.

He stirred and watched her, all calm and devastating, while she was internally making lists; he knew what she was doing.

"You're staring and thinking too hard."

She smiled. "Am not."

"You are. I can feel it."

She propped herself on an elbow, mock offended. "I'm recalibrating my entire adult identity, actually."

His eyes opened. "That sounds stressful."

"It is. Also, you're very distracting."

"Good," he said, his voice still half-asleep. "Then stop thinking."

She laughed. "You don't make it easy."

He reached for her hand, pulled her closer until her head fit perfectly in the curve of his shoulder. "Wasn't supposed to be easy."

And that was that.

They kissed again, slowly, the kind of kiss that felt less like starting something and more like remembering how to breathe.

That was all it took to bring last night rushing back, the bar, the word *Stay*, the kiss that had rewritten her body's entire language.

They moved without choreography. A tangle of morning skin, quiet laughter, the soft sound of sheets shifting.

"I think this is the first time you haven't tried to plan the next thing," he said.

She tilted her head. "Maybe I'm learning."

He smiled into her shoulder. "Dangerous habit."

She put on his hoodie, the sleeves were too long, the fabric smelt of Nico. She wanted to crawl back into bed and freeze time.

They ate breakfast together. The scrambled eggs had that suspicious hotel sheen that screamed powdered assistance, the toast had cooled into a pale version of itself, and one of the jam portions had exploded somewhere between the kitchen and the room, coating the inside of the lid like a crime scene.

They sat cross-legged on the bed, the tray between them, both of them poking at the food without much commitment.

"This is probably a metaphor," she said.

He glanced over, bemused. "You think we're cold toast and undercooked eggs?"

He reached over and wiped a smear of jam from the corner of her mouth.

"You know," he added, "I didn't think we'd get here."

"Here, as in... this hotel room?"

"Here as in any version of 'after.'"

Sienna looked down at the crumpled napkin in her lap. "Me either."

They sat in the stillness, surrounded by overpriced toast and soft sheets and a city that hadn't yet asked anything of them that morning.

"Now you're stealing my jam, and I'm wearing your hoodie."

He nodded thoughtfully. "So, we're calling this progress."

They smiled. That slow, smile people wear when they know the walls aren't coming back up.

The tray had been cleared. The bed was remade more or less. Nico had gone to shower. Her phone buzzed from the nightstand. Olivia. Of course.

"Still alive? Or should I start planning the funeral?"

Sienna smirked. *"He's still here."*

Three blinking dots. Then:

"Like… in the room? Or metaphorically? Because I need to know whether to open the wine or call security."

Sienna tried not to laugh out loud. *"Physically. Emotionally. All of it. He stayed."*

A longer pause.

"Oh god. It happened. The worst-case scenario."
"What's that?" Sienna replied.
"Feelings. Now I'm going to have to respect him, aren't I?" Olivia asked.
"Yes. Sorry."
"Ugh. Fine."
Sienna let out a laugh, the kind that made her cover her mouth and glance toward the bathroom, even though she had nothing to hide. The door to the bathroom opened, and Nico stepped out, towelling off his hair, shirtless. Now that was a Kodak moment she wanted to remember forever. Sienna tossed her phone aside and rose from the bed like she wasn't balancing on the edge of something that felt dangerously like joy. She tried not to stare at him.
She tried not to beam.

They got up eventually, dressing and pretending not to watch each other in the mirror. She ordered coffee; he found music. Nothing remarkable, except that it was. Sienna went to the window in one of his shirts, watching the city stir awake. Taxis. Steam rising from vents. Somewhere, a siren. He joined her quietly, mug in hand, hair still a mess, the kind of morning sight that could stop time if she let it. He smiled, then looked around the suite. He leaned his shoulder against hers. "So how long are we going to pretend this hotel is our house?"
She looked up at him. "We'll figure it out. New York's big enough for two people who have no idea what they're doing, you're staying?"
He didn't hesitate. "Already did."
The words sat between them, steady as a heartbeat.

The knock came just after noon. Three polite raps. A pause. Then another. Sienna glanced at him. "You expecting someone?"
He shook his head, still buttoning his shirt. Sienna frowned, crossing the room. She opened the door to find a young concierge in the doorway holding a thick cream envelope.

"Ms Hartley?"

"Yes."

"This was left at reception. Hand-delivered. No return name, but they said it was urgent."

The handwriting across the front was unmistakable. Marc's careful slant.

"Thank you," she said, and closed the door.

Nico was leaning against the counter, watching her. "Who's it from?"

She turned the envelope over, thumb brushing the edge. "Marc."

Nico watched the movement of her hand. "Do you want me to stay?"

She looked up. "I don't know yet."

He stepped closer, brushing his fingers along her arm, light as static. "Then I'll be wherever you need me."

That was the thing about him. He didn't ask to read it. He trusted her to decide how to face it. Sienna sat on the edge of the bed, broke the seal, and unfolded the pages.

Sienna,

I didn't want to bother you, but you've been on my mind.

Of course, she had. That was always how it started. Never with accountability, Marc always demanded access, only on his terms; he never barged in, he slipped through cracks. Cracks he created, then blamed her for.

I walked past that Thai place you used to hate last week. It's a sushi place now. You were right, it was always terrible.

Charming. Trying to be familiar. Nostalgic bait designed to lower her guard. She kept reading.

I still think about our weekends. How we'd sleep until noon and pretend we weren't checking our phones under the covers. You were always smarter than me at pretending not to care.

There it was, the pivot. The guilt-as-flattery.

I know I didn't always handle things well. I know I let work eat everything. But I never stopped thinking of you as the person I'd eventually come back to.

Sienna felt her jaw tighten. The person I'd eventually come back to. Like she was a fallback plan. A default setting.

I see your name everywhere now. The articles. The panels. You've always been the smartest person in every room. I just wish I'd told you that before you stopped needing to hear it.

Apology by omission. Compliment as manipulation. A final line with a hook. Still, she read the last part.

You've always been brilliant at reinventing yourself, and you always needed to prove you could do it without me. I suppose now you have. I only wish I'd been part of the version that finally worked. I'll be at the Mercer until Friday. No pressure. But if you want to talk, I'll be in the corner booth. You always said that was your spot."

Marc.

She sat still for a few seconds, just that cold, familiar weight in her chest that she had hoped to outgrow. Marc hadn't changed. But she had. Marc's tone was exactly as she remembered: elegant, self-aware, dripping with uninvited nostalgia. She read it twice. Her jaw clenched. When she looked up, Nico was leaning against the wall, watching her carefully. She folded the letter once, then again, and said quietly, "I need air." She passed it to him. "You can read it if you want."

He took it, unfolded it, and read it. Then carefully folded it again and set it on the coffee table. Just one question. "What do you want to do with it?" She stared at the envelope. Her name in his handwriting. All sharp angles and ownership. And suddenly, the answer was clear.

"Rooftop?" He asked.

"Yes", she replied.

They didn't speak much on the way to the rooftop; the wind tugged at her hair. The skyline glared - hard, bright, and beautiful. Sienna held the letter in one hand; Nico's hoodie draped over her other arm. She crouched down beside an ashtray and held the letter over a lighter she borrowed from a stranger smoking near the railing.

"I used to keep them all," she said. "Every note. Every apology. Proof that someone once thought I mattered."

Nico waited beside her. "This one is different?"

"Yes," she said, her eyes meeting his. "I don't need the proof anymore. I know I matter." She replied.

She flicked the lighter. The flame caught the corner of the page, turned it gold, then black. Words curled, then vanished. Marc's name went last. When the ashes settled, she brushed her hands clean, knocking the last of him into the wind. Sienna exhaled like she'd been holding her breath since Barcelona. Below them, the city shimmered, restless, bright, alive. He touched her back lightly. "Feel better?"

"Not better. Clearer." She straightened, the wind off the Hudson cutting through the heat of the fire.

"That's enough." He reached for her hand, his fingers anchoring her. They walked to the edge and looked out. There was the smell of burnt paper, the hum of eight million people, and, for the first time, a horizon that didn't look like a threat.

"Do you still have a flight?" she asked.

He smiled, faint but certain. "I cancelled it this morning."

She turned to him. "Before the letter?"

"Before the coffee."

The moment filled itself. Below them, the city kept moving, a thousand small stories unfolding at once. Nico squeezed her hand.

"Come on. Let's see if the world still makes room for us."

She looked at him, the city lights cutting across his face, and for the first time since she could remember, she didn't think about what came next. They walked inside together, the door closing behind them, completely, like a beginning that had been waiting its turn.

Chapter Twenty-Three

THE MEETING

She didn't need to be convinced. That was the difference this time. There was no pacing or a crisis playlist. No talking to herself in the mirror like a woman about to walk into a firing squad. Sienna Hartley was getting dressed for a meeting, and for once, it didn't feel like an audition.

The outfit was deliberate. Tailored trousers, a royal purple blouse, blazer with sharp shoulders. Hair up glossy and sleek, she was not trying to impress or conform; she wanted to define herself on her terms. Her phone buzzed as she slipped on her earrings. It was Olivia.

"You in full boss mode yet, or do you need me to remind you how underqualified those in the room will be?"

Sienna smiled.

"Already ahead of you. Blazer's on. Confidence pending."

"You're not there to be discovered. You're there to decide if they're worth discovering. Now go. Make at least one of them nervous," Olivia replied.

Sienna tucked her phone into her bag and glanced toward the other side of the room. Nico had gone out for a walk. He'd offered to come with her, wait in the café downstairs, but she'd said no. Not because she didn't want him there - because this moment was hers. And yet, a whisper in her mind reminded her that whatever happened in this meeting would ripple outward. Into her time. Into the small, new world she and Nico were building.

She took a breath. This wasn't about choosing between love and ambition. It was about choosing what kind of life she wanted. Not the life she used to chase or the one she built out of damage control, but the one she'd only just begun to imagine.

The car ride over was calm; there were no nervous butterflies, just clarity. The agency's office was exactly as she expected - glass walls, shaped succulents, the faint scent of toner and ambition. Coffee-table books stacked with surgical precision. Everyone smiled just a little too much. At the reception, a woman with a headset glanced up.

"Ms Hartley? They're ready for you."

Of course they were.

She checked her reflection in the brass panel beside the elevator, one last look. The doors opened. She stepped in and let them close behind her. They were already seated when she walked in. Three of them. Two men, one woman, all styled within an inch of their PR budgets. Laptops open. Sparkling water poured.

"Sienna, thank you so much for coming," said the man on the left. Mid-forties, high-end watch, voice like a smooth pitch deck. Probably named Grant. "We've been looking forward to this."

"Of course," she said, shaking hands as they offered them. She didn't overdo it. Firm, polite and unrevealing.

She took the chair at the head of the table without being directed. Let them rearrange around her.

The woman with a sharp bob, even sharper heels, spoke next.

"We're huge fans of your work. The New Yorker piece was phenomenal. And that podcast you guest-hosted last year so clear, so bold."

Sienna gave a slight nod. "Thanks."

She didn't rush to fill the space. People underestimate how powerful it is to sit with your own presence.

The younger man leaned forward, bright with self-assurance.

"We see a real trajectory here. You've built something with integrity. That's rare and marketable."

There it was. Marketable.

They launched into the pitch. Exposure, partnerships, audience expansion. She caught phrases like "cross-platform synergy" and "brand elasticity." Someone mentioned a book deal, a docuseries. They had it all mapped out, how to take her voice and shape it into something with "scale."

She sat back, watching them talk *at* her like she was an algorithm. She let it run for a full five minutes before lifting her hand slightly.

"I have a question," she said calmly.

They stopped talking, and all eyes snapped to her.

"If you hadn't seen my name in headlines, would I be sitting here?"

"Well, of course, we seek out meaningful work", the young one said.

"No," she interrupted. "Would I be sitting here if I weren't already visible?"

The woman recovered first. "We'd like to think we're ahead of the curve when it comes to recognising talent."

Sienna smiled. "You're not. You're late."

Then came the name-drop.

"I actually worked with Marc for a while," said Grant, casually flipping a pen through his fingers. "Back when he was still at Vero. Brilliant guy. Really respected your dynamic."

Her spine straightened a fraction.

"Marc respected Marc," she said. "The rest of us were scenery."

He gave an uncertain laugh, unsure whether it was a joke. She didn't clarify. Sienna let the awkward moment return. And this time, no one rushed to fill it. The energy shifted. Sienna felt it like a tide turning.

"You've all talked a lot about audience," she said. "Exposure. Alignment. But what I haven't heard is anything about value."

"Meaning…?" Grant ventured.

"Meaning, what is it *you* see in me that isn't already seen? What's the gap you think you're filling?"

They hesitated. She didn't.

"Because what I'm hearing is the same offer I've always turned down, curation without clarity. Visibility without intention."

The younger man shifted in his seat and tried again.

"We see the opportunity to evolve your brand. To take what you've done and."

She smiled and cut in. "I'm not a startup."

"No, of course not. But there's room to"

She cut him off again, "There's always room. Doesn't mean I want to live in it."

The woman adjusted her blouse. "Ms Hartley, we're not trying to control your narrative. We're here to help you grow it."

"Are you?"

Silence again, and this time, they felt it too. She reached into her bag, unfolded the conference schedule and laid it flat.

"They've asked me to give the opening keynote."

The woman leaned in, reading the header. "That's a huge platform."

"It is. And I haven't said yes yet."

"Why not?" the young man asked.

Sienna looked at him squarely. "Because I wanted to see if this room would make me feel surer of who I am… or less."

Grant leaned back. The charm was flickering now. "And?"

"I'm still deciding."

She pushed back her chair. "I'll leave you to discuss your alignment."

The woman rose to her feet, flustered. "We'd love to send you a revised proposal"

"Do that."

She gathered her things. "Thank you for the sparkling water."

And just like that, she walked out.

The hallway was brighter than it had any right to be. Her heels clicked against marble - the same rhythm she'd once faked for confidence. Only now, it was real. She was halfway to the lift when she heard footsteps behind her.

"Ms Hartley, Sienna, wait."

It was Grant…

He jogged slightly to catch up, all smooth charm suddenly softened by panic. Like he'd just realised something precious might slip through his fingers.

"I hope we didn't give the wrong impression," he said, panting lightly. "It's hard to cover everything in a first meeting, especially with someone at your level."

She turned, patient but unyielding.

"You gave exactly the impression I expected," she said. "That's the problem."

He flinched, only slightly. "We weren't trying to reduce your voice to a product."

"No," she agreed, "but you were trying to *package* it. Same thing. Different spin."

He tried again. "We're offering options. Control. Leverage."

"I already have leverage," she said calmly. "You just didn't notice."

She handed him her card. Grant hesitated.

"If you're serious," she said, "you'll follow up with something that *actually* sees me. If not, don't worry - I have options."

He took the card; she turned and walked toward the lift.

No looking back. She didn't need to win the room. She had *left* the room.

In the elevator, her reflection stared back from the brass doors. This wasn't about walking out for effect. It was about walking out *before she compromised.* She stepped into the lobby and pulled out her phone. One new message waited.

It was Nico. *"Coffee in the lounge. Unless it's terrible. In which case, rescue me."*
She smiled. Typed back:
"Be there in five."

She didn't leave because she was angry. She left because she was done pretending to be impressed by rooms that only saw her value once it became visible to everyone else.
That version of her, the one who used to twist herself into something palatable, easier to pitch, wasn't coming back.
And she didn't need a dramatic ending. She just needed a clean one.

As the revolving doors of the agency spilled her into daylight, she breathed in the crisp city air. It felt *clarifying*, so she walked.
A man passed her on the footpath, mumbling into his phone. A woman was crying by the bus stop, mascara smudged, but shoulders held high. Everyone was living their story, and so was she. And hers didn't start in that boardroom. It didn't end there, either.
She pulled her blazer tighter. Straightened her spine. And walked back toward the hotel, not as someone with a decision to make, but as someone who already had.

⚷
TSR

Inside the hotel lounge, Nico sat in the corner, legs stretched out, unread *Paris Review* in hand. He spotted her before she spotted him.
She didn't say anything as she walked over, just raised a brow.
He closed the magazine and gave her a look.
"That face," he said as she approached, "either you walked out mid-pitch… or someone offered you a reality show."
Sienna dropped her bag onto the chair opposite and sat down.

"Close. They tried to turn me into a brand."

He winced. "Ooo."

"They said 'scale' three times in five minutes and someone name-dropped Marc."

Nico grimaced. "Ah. The final boss of mansplaining."

She let out a short laugh. It surprised her how easily it came. The weight of the meeting hadn't disappeared, but it no longer sat like stone on her chest.

He nudged the espresso toward her. "Want it? It's not terrible. But it's definitely not good."

She took a sip and wrinkled her nose. "You're right. This is aggressively mediocre."

"Great band name."

The soft clink of cutlery from the café. A child laughing nearby. The kind of background noise that doesn't ask anything of you.

Then he asked it.

"Did you get what you wanted?"

She looked down at the table. Traced the rim of the cup with her finger.

"No."

She looked up. "But I think I got what I needed."

He nodded. "There's a difference."

"Yeah. Turns out chasing the wrong thing still feels like progress until you stop."

He leaned forward, elbows on knees. "So. What now?"

She paused.

"I say yes to the keynote," she said. "Not because it looks good on paper. Because it scares me in the right way."

Nico didn't speak for a second. Then:

"Will it make you happy?"

That stopped her.

He wasn't trying to convince her. Wasn't offering safety or redirection.

Just a question that held space.

"I think so." She said.

He relaxed back into the chair. "Then I vote yes."

She smiled. "Oh, is that how it works?"

"No. But I still like being consulted."

She raised her espresso cup like a toast. "To reckless decisions made with suspicious clarity."

He raised his water glass. "And to men who don't panic when you make them."

Their glasses clinked. And for the first time in a long, long while, Sienna didn't feel like she had to apologise for wanting more.

They decided to walk; the sun was starting to fall sideways through the buildings, casting long shadows across the pavement, gold-edged, forgiving. The city looked less like a threat and more like a place you could start over in if you weren't too proud to try again.

At the corner, Nico's hand brushed against hers. Neither pulled away.

They stopped at a red light near the corner of Houston.

"I kept thinking it would feel bigger," she said, eyes on the blinking pedestrian sign.

"What would?"

"Walking out. Turning them down. Choosing something unknown instead of something *certain*." She glanced at him. "But it didn't feel triumphant. It just felt… right."

He smiled. "When you know, you know."

At the hotel entrance, Nico held the door for her. She walked in first but slowed just enough for him to fall in beside her.

The suite was still made up. Room service had passed through, pillows fluffed, glasses replaced, and an unnecessary orchid repositioned to the centre of the table.

Nico loosened his shirt cuffs and sat on the edge of the bed.

Sienna dropped her bag on the armchair and kicked off her heels and joined him.

"I don't know what the future holds," she said finally. "The speaking thing. Us. Any of it."

"Me neither."

"I'm used to answers. Deadlines. Outcomes." She was still wired from the meeting. "This feels like standing on a bridge with no railing."

"Then don't look down." He said.

She turned to him, her expression guarded but soft. "And if I fall?"

He shrugged. "Then I'll catch you. Or I'll fall too. Either way, at least we'll know what the hell we're doing."

It was absurd. Romantic. Utterly reckless and perfect all at the same time. She laughed. A real, unfiltered laugh that cracked through her exhaustion and pulled something loose in her chest. And for once, she didn't feel the need to second-guess it.

Nico offered his hand. "Come on."

"Where are we going?"

"Somewhere that serves actual wine, not minibar guilt."

She raised a brow. "Is this a celebration?"

"No," he said. "This is a Wednesday."

She took his hand.

At the door, she turned to look back at the suite, just aware that something had shifted inside its walls. That a version of her had taken shape here. And another had been left behind.

Then she stepped into the hallway, a woman walking into a life she was finally designing on purpose.

Chapter Twenty-Four

THE PHOTO

Olivia was early, or maybe Sienna was late. Either way, she found herself alone at the hotel bar with a half-poured glass of wine and the sort of lull that usually meant something was about to happen.
Her expression often held a dry, unimpressed quality, but it would occasionally break with a quick, almost mischievous smile that disappeared as fast as it appeared.

She had a sharp, clipped way of speaking, a tone that could cut through noise or nonsense with polite precision. She would observe others from the edge of a conversation, a smirk playing on her lips, only stepping in with a perfectly timed and devastatingly witty remark.
She was also a chameleon. That was the best way to describe her. One day her hair was a warm, honeyed brown, the next a striking, cool blonde that seemed to amplify her eyes. She was the kind of person who could command a room with a look or a single, thoughtfully chosen sentence. She could be the polished, collected figure in a tailored suit one moment, and a slightly dishevelled but fiercely determined hero the next, with an easy confidence in either role.

She scanned the room. There was a gold light, sleek interiors; it was the kind of place that pretended not to care how expensive everything was. She reached for her phone, but something on the back shelf behind the bar caught her eye.

A small frame, made of black wood, was half-tucked between a stack of cocktail books and an unused decanter.

Olivia squinted. "Hey," she called casually to the bartender. "What's that photo?"

He turned, followed her gaze, then shrugged. "Been there a while. Someone left it behind, we think. A guest, they never claimed it."

She walked closer.

The photo was black and white and had softened with time. A woman stood in front of what looked like a stone church, coat blowing slightly in the wind, hands deep in her pockets. There was something in her expression, even in monochrome, guarded and complicated.

Olivia felt her heart shift sideways.

She leaned in closer, the bar noise slipping away until it was just her and the photograph.

"My god," she whispered, the corners of her mouth tilting. "Of course it's her."

It wasn't recognition in the usual sense; it was realisation. Like finding the origin story of someone you thought you already understood.

It was Sienna.

A younger version, possibly early-twenties, her hair a bit longer, face sharper, but unmistakably her.

She didn't look posed at all; she looked caught, like someone had been watching her and knew exactly when to press the shutter.

Olivia turned to the bartender again. "You're sure this was left behind?"

"That's what we were told. Someone from the fourth-floor suite brought it down. Said it was found in a drawer."

Suite, fourth floor.

Olivia shook her head, a knowing smile tugging at her mouth. Of course, it was Nico.

She looked at it, hands by her side. The photo wasn't nostalgic or romantic; it was something heavier, it felt much deeper. Like proof of something Olivia hadn't even known Sienna had lost.

She reached out, lifted it carefully, and felt the strange tightness in her shoulders that only came when something was important.

"Thanks," she said. "I'll return it."

The bartender nodded, already distracted by a group of tourists ordering champagne.

Olivia sat back down, photo resting face-up beside her wine.

Sienna had no idea this existed. But he'd kept it. Nico had actually *kept* it. And not just in his wallet or tucked inside a book. He left it in his suite, in this hotel, where Sienna had returned to him, to whatever the hell this whole thing was.

This wasn't about longing for each other; this was about memory, maybe even destiny.

Olivia sipped her wine, looked at the photo again, and smiled.

"Oh, babe," she murmured. "You have no idea."

Olivia held the photo like it was a page from someone else's diary, very personal and fragile; it was not hers to interpret, but somehow hers to deliver.

She waited another few minutes, half-hoping Sienna would arrive before she changed her mind. But no noise came from her phone; there was one unread text from Marc still unopened and an Instagram ad trying to sell her a weighted blanket "for emotionally intelligent women."

She snorted and drained the rest of her wine.

"Excuse me," she said to the bartender again, holding up the photo now. "Do you know who actually brought this down?"

He looked up from slicing lime. "The suite cleaner said it was left behind. The guest didn't claim it, so the manager just told us to hold it in case someone asked."

"No guest name?"

He shook his head.

But Olivia already knew. She didn't need a name.

There weren't many men who'd take a photo like that, not just *of* someone, but *for* them. The framing was too intimate; it was precise, not particularly romantic at all, but very deliberate.

She imagined Nico slipping it into his suitcase years ago, carrying it city to city. Keeping it close by, not taking it out to show anyone or framing it, keeping it safe.

Maybe he'd wanted to give it to Sienna. Maybe he thought the moment had passed, or maybe he couldn't let go, even when she had.

Olivia traced the edge of the frame with her finger.

Sienna never talked about that trip in detail. She only mentioned Barcelona once, years ago, drunk on a rooftop with too much gin and not enough sense and of course, the recent revelation.

"Some places," she'd said, "aren't meant to be revisited."

Olivia had never pushed for details, even though she wanted all of them. Now she knew it had been more than she realised - especially after Sienna told her about the baby.

Now, here it was. The memory Sienna had buried, preserved by someone who'd never stopped seeing her, *even when she stopped looking at herself.*

Frame in hand, she left a twenty on the bar. Sienna didn't come to the bar, so she had to go to Sienna.

As she walked toward the lift, Olivia rehearsed what she'd say.

"Look what I found."

"Guess who never forgot?"

Or maybe just: *"You're going to want to sit down."*

But none of it felt right, because this wasn't a story, it was a mirror, and sometimes, you don't narrate a reflection. You just hold it up.

The suite door clicked open, but Olivia didn't step in right away.

She waited in the threshold, holding the photo, she took a deep breath, and decided to use her instinct alone.

Inside, Sienna was curled on the window seat, knees tucked under her, a half-filled journal resting across her thighs. The pen uncapped and the page blank.

She looked up, surprised.

"Hey. Sorry, am I late, or are you early?"

Olivia didn't answer. She just walked in, closed the door gently behind her, and crossed the room.

Sienna straightened a little. "Everything ok?"

Olivia stopped in front of her. Said nothing. Held out the photo, both hands.

Sienna blinked and took it.

She stared at it for so long that Olivia thought maybe she didn't recognise herself.

But then something changed in her expression. It wasn't shock or confusion, but a sense of heaviness, as if her face folded inward, pressing against something old, soft, and scarred. Her fingers brushed the corner of the frame.

The feeling had changed. It felt heavier now. Sienna looked up. Her voice was quieter than Olivia had heard in days.

"Where did you find this?"

"Bar." Olivia sat next to her. "It was behind the shelf. The bartender said someone found it in a suite, so they held onto it just in case."

She didn't say which suite. She didn't need to.

Sienna's eyes were still on the photo.

"That day…" she began, then trailed off.

Olivia remained patient and waited for Sienna to take it all in. Sienna ran her finger across the surface of the glass.

"It was windy. I remember that. I was trying to look confident, and instead I looked like I wanted to disappear."

"Well, you didn't because there you are."

"I did," Sienna said, almost absently. "Back then, I didn't think I was worth remembering. Let alone photographing."

She kept staring at the girl in the picture, the one who had no idea she was being seen, *really* seen, through someone else's lens. Preserved without consent or warning. And somehow, without distortion.

She wasn't smiling in the photo. But she wasn't hiding either.

She looked *real*.

Sienna swallowed.

"He kept it?"

"Looks like it," Olivia replied quietly.

Sienna exhaled slowly. Like letting out a truth she'd been holding in for years.

She held the photograph to her chest; it was as if the individual depicted, the version of herself in the coat, hair windswept, was worthy of acknowledgment and care.

Olivia reached out and rested her warm hand on hers.

"You don't have to say anything," she said.

"I know."

But Sienna did say something.

"Maybe I wasn't lost. I just forgot where to look."

Olivia squeezed her hand once more before she left, eyes soft but teasing. "Then maybe it's time you stopped searching for proof."

Sienna stayed by the window. The city seemed dimmer than it once was, as the light grew softer and less intense. Dusk had crept in like a secret.

She turned the photo over in her hands, as if it might reveal something on the back. There was nothing there, only the smooth, matte finish of time.

But the memory was there. Lurking just beneath the surface, sharp and clear.

Barcelona.

The church wasn't famous or a landmark. It was a building on a street they'd stumbled into while trying to find an ATM. Her coat had been too warm. Her hair kept whipping into her eyes. And Nico twenty-something, bold, impossibly earnest, had stopped in his tracks.

"Don't move," he'd said, lifting the camera.

She'd laughed, turned away. "Why? I look awful."

He pressed the shutter anyway. Not because she looked perfect, but because something in her expression broke him open. She was both leaving and staying in that moment, and he wanted proof that he hadn't imagined her.

She hadn't thought about that moment again. She'd buried it like the rest of that summer under responsibility, reinvention, and the kind of silence that grows teeth.

But now it was in her hands. Proof. Not just that it happened, but that it mattered to someone other than her.

She set the photo on the windowsill and leaned back against the glass. She let the memory stretch out, like film unspooling, each frame clearer than the last.

She remembered what it felt like to be seen by him. How terrifying that was. And how badly she'd wanted it.

And she remembered why she'd left.

Because wanting wasn't enough.

She'd been too young to trust it. Too afraid to believe she could be both vulnerable and whole. She thought she had to choose.

Now, decades later, the same man had handed her a room key with no explanation, no expectation, only a second chance.

And he'd kept this photo the whole time.

She finally cried.

The tears came in a single, clean line down her cheek. No shaking shoulders or gasps.

Just the release of someone who finally understood she hadn't been invisible after all.

She wiped her face and laughed, softly.

It wasn't the sadness that got her. It was the grace.

She picked up the photo again. Held it at eye level.

"I see you now," she whispered.

And meant it.

Nico found her on the window seat, the lights dimmed low, the city curling itself into the night behind her. The photo rested in her lap now, but she didn't move when he stepped in. She just looked at him like she was still catching up to everything she'd just realised.

He didn't ask what was wrong.

He sat beside her, like he knew the air was thick with something sacred. His thigh pressed gently against hers, warm and steady. His presence didn't ask. It offered.

She passed him the photo without a word.

Nico took it. Looked at it like it was something familiar to him, part of him.

"Didn't think you'd ever see that," he said.

Sienna exhaled, a small sound that was almost a laugh. "I didn't even know it existed."

He turned it over, then back. "I didn't plan to take it. You just looked… like you were holding something together with everything you had."

"I was," she whispered.

Their eyes met, and rather than being overwhelmed by the past, she found it provided clarity and perspective.

"You kept it?" she asked, softly.

"For a long time."

"Why?"

He smiled genuinely, without any hint of pretence; his expression conveyed sincerity.

"Because I wanted to remember what it looked like the exact second I knew you were going to leave."

There was no reaction from the room, nor from her.

That should have hurt. But instead, it was received gently, like he wasn't blaming her, only honouring what had been.

She stared at the photo again. Her younger self, frozen mid-breath, eyes unreadable.

"I didn't think I was worth being remembered," she said. "Back then. I thought being loved meant being fixed."

Nico didn't rush her. His hand moved to hers, stroking lightly across the top.

"What about now?"

She didn't answer right away. Instead, she leaned into him, slightly to share the weight.

"I'm learning," she said. "That maybe I don't need to be seen perfectly. Just as me."

He kissed her temple softly, deliberately.

"That's what I've always done."

She looked at him, really looked. The lines near his eyes, the steady calm in the way he waited. The way he never once tried to tell her what she felt only made space for it.

And something in her cracked. In the best, gentlest way.

The part of her that had been acting even here, even now, finally sat down.

She walked to her journal. Removed the photo from the frame and slid it between two pages.

"Just need to see it, one last time."

Then she closed the book. And turned back to him.

They didn't go out that night. No rooftop drinks or dinner reservations. The city buzzed on without them, neon signs flickering promises they didn't need fulfilled. Instead, they stayed in. Sienna sat on the bed, knees bent, hair loosely tied. Nico was beside her, one leg dangling off the edge, shirt rumpled from hours of simply being still.

"I used to think love had to look like something," she said, eyes fixed on a spot across the room. "Big moments. Grand gestures. Explanations."

He didn't interrupt.

"But I'm realising…" She turned to face him. "It's this, too. The being seen. Not having to apologise for who you were before."

Nico tilted his head. "You were never someone who needed fixing Sienna."

Sienna smirked. "No, but I needed to believe that. You couldn't do that part for me."

"Didn't try."

"I know."

He leaned back on his palms, watching her like the city didn't exist outside these walls.

There was something in the moment, *not* a lack of words, but the presence of peace. Like they didn't need to fill the space anymore.

She crawled closer, legs crossing over his. Her fingers slid beneath his shirt at the hem, palm resting lightly on his stomach, connected.

"This feels like the part they leave out," she murmured. "In the movies. In the books. The after part."

Nico's hand found hers. "That's because the after part's the point."

They kissed then slowly, deep, like they'd finally arrived in the same version of the story.

And when they broke apart, foreheads resting against each other, Sienna felt it.

This is reality, not a fairytale.

Her body wasn't perfect. Her past wasn't neat. But she was here. *Fully.*

She was no longer pretending to be someone else, no longer bracing for impact; she was now becoming.

She let out a breath she hadn't realised she'd been holding since
Barcelona.

"I cried today," she said softly.

Nico looked at her, waiting.

"Not because I was sad," she added. "But because I finally saw myself."

He reached up, brushed a strand of hair behind her ear. "Took you
long enough."

She laughed, the sound catching mid-throat.

"Shut up."

She kissed him again; there was no narrative necessity, she chose to do
so, and she really wanted to.

The suite had grown darker, but neither of them reached for the light.
Eventually, Sienna stretched, letting the moment settle into something
lived in. Her bare feet padded across the carpet to the bathroom. She
wasn't fleeing, just moving, freely, like her body no longer carried
invisible weights.

In the mirror, she caught her reflection. She looked. Held eye contact
with herself. Let her shoulders drop.

There she was. Wrinkled shirt. Smudged mascara. Lip bitten from
nerves or kissing, she couldn't tell which.

She wasn't edited-beautiful anymore - she was the kind of beautiful that
happens when light lands somewhere it finally recognises.

Behind her, Nico appeared in the doorway. He leaned against the
frame, arms crossed, watching without invading.

"Is that how you see yourself now?" he asked gently.

She smiled at her reflection. "It's closer."

He crossed the room, slow and barefoot. Wrapped his arms around her
from behind, his chest warm against her spine.

They stood like that for a while. Two people who had once fallen apart
without ever having a real fight. Now choosing to stay, not because of
some dramatic plea, but because *this* made sense.

"Thank you," she said.

"For what?"

"For never calling it love when I couldn't return it."

He kissed her shoulder.

"You don't owe me anything," he replied. "But I think you're about to give me everything anyway." And smiled.

She turned in his arms. Pressed her lips to his, soft, assured.

Her phone buzzed, ruining the moment.

She checked it.

It was a text from Olivia. "*I swear, if you two are blissed out and emotionally evolved and don't tell me every detail over brunch tomorrow, I'm staging a one-woman dramatic reenactment of your relationship with props. And tears. So many fake tears.*"

Sienna laughed aloud, the sound catching Nico's attention.

"What?" he asked.

She held up the phone. "That was a threat."

Nico grinned. "She terrifies me."

"Ha, Good."

She set the phone down, stepped back into him, and rested her head against his chest.

The night could have ended in a dozen ways: champagne, declarations, sex. But it didn't need to. They were already here.

Enough - that was the point all along.

Chapter Twenty-Five

THE BEGINNING

"Three minutes," the stage manager said.

She touched two fingers to her wrist. One breath. Then another. Suite 2 rose in her mind like a photo: a thin stripe of light across sheets, the shape of a shoulder, the way a room sounds when you stop bracing.

"Ready?" the stage manager asked.

"Yes."

The keynote wasn't flawless, but it was hers. She spoke about the rise of artificial intelligence in content creation, the shift to short-form video, and the need to navigate it all through authenticity. She talked about cutting through ad fatigue and mistrust, and ended with her own story, fear, control, and the relief of finally staying true to herself. When she finished, the applause felt like quiet recognition more than noise. She bowed her head, and the stage manager gave a thumbs-up. The mic clicked mute. As she stepped into the wings, she saw him. He was there where the curtain gathered, hands in his pockets, eyes holding hers like a lifeline. He looked at her as if he had been holding a line taut and could finally let it ease.

"Hi," he said.

"Hi." She smiled.

He lifted his camera and took one frame.

Click.

The foyer churned. Programs, handshakes and thanks. Olivia appeared, sliding in like a blade wrapped in silk, her hair in a sleek, low knot, cheekbones catching the light, a tailored jacket that knew how to hang from a shoulder.

"You caused a small ethical crisis in row four," she murmured. "She is currently re-evaluating a boyfriend, a job and a haircut. Inspiring day."
"Three for one," Sienna said. "Efficient. Any survivors?"
"A few. The rest are in recovery."

A tall man in all-black who had the forearms of a person who lifts trusses before breakfast, had a coil of tape hooked to his belt, and eyes that kept finding the light sources in the room without meaning to, was in such a rush to get the venue ready for a private event, he ran straight into Sienna and Olivia.

"Oh my god, I'm so sorry!" he said. He brushed himself off and offered his hand. "Theo, nice to meet you."
Olivia accepted it before Sienna could. "Olivia." Her mouth tilted, and her eyebrow raised. "Was that your opening move, or are you saving the rest for later?"
"No," he grinned, "Usually I start with lighting cues, not collisions."

She looked him over, amused approval hidden under professionalism. "Efficient, though," she replied. "You get contact and conversation in one hit."
"Then I'll call it creative problem-solving."
"You'd get along with me, then."
"That's the plan?" he asked.
She blushed. "I'm considering it."
Theo's laugh had that low, effortless sound of someone who didn't need to try. Olivia lingered a half-step closer than necessary.

"We'll see you downstairs," she said to Sienna, eyes still on Theo.

"Or not," Sienna replied.

Olivia's grin was quick and knowing. "Probably not."

She turned back to Theo. "Come on, show me these lighting cues you're so proud of."

Sienna shook her head, half-smiling, and started toward the side corridor that led to the loading dock. The hum of post-event chatter faded behind her, replaced by the low rhythm of rain on the awning outside.

Nico was waiting there, watching the city shift through the glass doors. He turned as she approached; the kind of look that made the room slow around him.

"You were incredible," he said.

"You heard it?"

"Every word."

He reached into his pocket and held out a small white envelope.

"What is this?" she asked.

"This isn't a grand gesture," he said. "But it's a good one, I hope?"

Inside were two keys on a plain ring and a small brass tag stamped:

Bowery Studio. Gate.

Her heart performed a small, private tilt as she turned the tag over with her thumb. "You rented a studio."

"For a season," he said. "Three months. I have a show in Madrid; I told them I am working from here until spring. There are flights both ways. There's no pressure, and I am not giving you an ultimatum, just a season. I want to see what our days look like when they are not borrowed."

Sienna closed her fingers around the keys. "A season," she repeated. "If it works, we extend. If it doesn't, we will know it was real and not pretend it was about schedules."

She smiled. "Come with me," she said.

They slipped out, past crates and cables, into a block washed in soft light. Cool air smelled faintly of rain that had changed its mind, and taxis sluiced past.

"Take me there," she said.

He understood without needing more words.

A man balanced a pastry box. A florist rinsed petals into the gutter. A child walked a low wall, a parent's hand hovering. The city was alive, the same pulse as their racing hearts.

The Bowery studio was three flights up in a narrow stairwell that had stored the echo of a thousand footsteps. The studio door was dented in the corners, which Sienna liked. Nico turned the key, and as they stepped inside, the room opened. Brick that had stopped pretending to be perfect. Two tall windows with southern light. A quiet hum in the bones of the place, like the aftersound of a cello. Air that had a clean, chalky taste. A paint-splattered stool. A single clean mug on a windowsill, nothing else.

"This will work," she said.

"For both of us?" he asked.

"For both of us," she said.

She walked to the nearest window, and he lifted his camera. She felt the impulse to pose and let it pass. She remained as she was, hair pushed back with the heel of her hand, shoulders square because she had decided they would be. She moved into the light and breathed until the room recognised her.

"Now," she said.

Click.

He lowered the camera. "This one is for the wall, not the drawer."

She crossed to him, took his hand and studied the raw space from his side. The glass held a reflection that layered them and scattered them. She could see a life form in the negative space.

"Show me the courtyard," she said.

The second key opened a small iron gate. A rectangle of trees that had learned to be kind in little soil, inside a square of worn brick. There was a bench with flaking paint and a string of bulbs that would make promises later.

They sat. He rested his hand on the back of the bench and looked up as if measuring the height of summer. They stayed until the light turned the walls the colour of a ripe pear. When they rose, he locked the gate with the second key and pressed it into her palm.

"This one is yours," he said.

TSR

They returned to the hotel as the day thinned into evening. Suite 2 felt like a room already exhaling them when they opened the door. Her conference badge waited on the console. The unnecessary orchid faced forward like a soldier who had never seen actual duty. The bed held the shape of a life in progress.

She crossed to the second room and stayed in the doorway as if greeting a person who had been patient. It had been a possibility, then a refuge, then proof. Now it felt like a threshold with nothing behind it that could scare her.

She stepped in and opened the wardrobe. On the top shelf sat her journal with a photograph tucked inside. She rested her palm on the cover and left it closed. She knew where it lived.

Nico leaned against the frame. "So," he said. "How does this end?"

"It doesn't," she said. "It keeps beginning."

He considered that, then smiled. "Hungry?"

"Yes."

"For what?"

"Everything," she said, and surprised herself by laughing.

They lay down on top of the covers and watched the ceiling. Sienna reached over and pulled the corner of the blanket back. Slid beneath it like she'd been doing this for years. Nico lay beside her; the ceiling above was plain. The hotel's ventilation system filled the background like white noise.

"I could stay like this for hours," she said.

They lay side by side for a while, eyes open, breaths steady. So still. Outside, the city carried on in its usual way, a late train rumbling underground, a soft thud of someone dropping something in the hallway. Sienna turned her head toward Nico. He was simply there. Present.

She sat up, drawing the blanket around her. The room felt like it had exhaled with her. A kind of softness she never trusted before, because it didn't come with a catch.

She glanced around, finally seeing it differently. The night didn't offer clarity. The sky didn't open with revelation. But in the silence of that room, in the breath between past and future, she felt something settle in her chest.

It wasn't certainty or relief. It was the gentle, weightless knowing that this is what love looks like now.

It waited. It wasn't the *second* room, or a backup plan. It was hers.

Not asking her to change.

Only glad she came.

⚷

TSR

Morning found them without alarms. Sienna woke first to the sensation of being exactly inside her life. She watched him for a moment, without worry or wariness but with curiosity.

This man. This moment was the answer she no longer needed to ask for.

She slid out of bed and wandered around the room; she wanted to be in it. To see it. Feel it.

Nico stirred, eyes still heavy. "You are up early," he said.

"I did not want to miss it."

"Miss what?"

"This," she said simply. "Waking up here. With this feeling."

He propped himself on an elbow, studying her. Sienna walked back over, climbed into bed, and tucked herself into the space beside him, as it belonged to her now.

They lay there like that for a while, two people who had finally arrived in the same place, at the same time.

Not because fate demanded it.

Because *they chose it.*

New York moved in its usual way, horns, footsteps, too many lives intersecting without meaning to.

They packed without talking about what it meant to pack. They dressed without being watched by the clock. She slipped her blazer over a T-shirt. He rolled his sleeves. They looked like people who had somewhere to go and were not rushing to get there.

"Your studio," she said. "I want to see it in morning light."

"Our studio," he said. "Then we start there."

When they were ready, she turned once more to the second room. She looked at it the way you nod to a place that kept you safe.

"Thank you," she said, quiet enough she could deny it later.

They left both keycards on the desk and closed the door. The second room did not hold them back.

Downstairs by the lifts, Olivia appeared, hair in a low knot, lipstick intact, heels in one hand, phone in the other. Theo followed with two coffees and the bashful grin of a man who had not slept much.

"Ahem, morning," Sienna said.

"Barely," Olivia answered, fastening her jacket. "I came to support you and accidentally got supported."

"You actually swiped right."

"Several times. Thorough research." She took one coffee from Theo, then eyed Sienna, smiling with a glint in her eye.

"You were good, Si. I love you. And by the way, that will do."

She gave a wink and tugged Theo's hand. "Breakfast and bad decisions, let's go."

Theo offered Sienna the spare coffee. "Congratulations," he said.

"Thanks."

"Oh, and by the way," Olivia said, turning back as the lift pinged. "I took that London job."

Sienna blinked. "You're serious?"

"Completely. Might even pack a winter coat this time."

She smiled. "Different continent, same story."

Then she was gone, they disappeared into the crowd, and Sienna smiled. Olivia didn't chase often. When she did, she usually caught it.

Outside, the city exhaled. Inside, she did too.
Nico was already across the street, talking and laughing with a woman, mid-thirties, camera strap slung over her shoulder.
On the sidewalk, a delivery bike swayed past with impossible pizzas. An older man watered a pot of rosemary with careful hands.
For a breath, that old ache rose, the one that always wrote endings before stories had a chance to begin.
See, he belongs elsewhere.
Then she noticed the gallery tag on the woman's tote, the quick professional handshake, and the way Nico's eyes found hers.
She made herself walk over.

"This is Lara," Nico said. "We worked together in Madrid."
"Good to meet you," Sienna said.
"Likewise," Lara replied, glancing between them with an almost-smile. "Ah… the photograph."

"What photograph?" Sienna asked.
"You'll see," Lara said, her voice kind, teasing. "He doesn't show his work unless it matters."
Nico shook his head, half-amused. "She never keeps secrets."
"That's why your exhibitions sell out," Lara said, then excused herself with a wave.

Sienna slipped her hand through Nico's arm.
"You ok?" he asked.
"I think so," she said, but there was a pulse of curiosity now, something that warmed beneath her ribs.
He smiled, small and sure. "Bowery?"

She nodded. "Let's go."

The studio was quiet when they arrived, the air still carrying the faint scent of fresh paint and dust. Their bags thudded softly onto the floor. Against the far wall, mounted in a simple black frame nearly two metres wide, hung the photograph - *her*, standing in the light of Suite 2, the moment he'd captured.

She stopped short. For a second, she didn't breathe.
"Nico…You had this printed?" she asked.
"I asked Lara to hang it while we were at the hotel," he said. "I wanted you to walk in and see what I see."
She turned to him, eyes glassy. "You always saw me like that?"
"Always," he said. "Even when you didn't."
She crossed to him and put her hands on his chest, palms flat, as if to steady the weight of what she felt.
"This was never about going back," she said. "It was about finally being met."
His forehead rested against hers. "Nice to meet you."

For a while, they remained there, quiet except for the low hum of the city through the windows. When she finally spoke, her voice was soft but certain.
"I love you," she said.
He brushed a strand of hair from her face. She leaned her forehead to his. Two people who had run out of reasons to leave.
"I've loved you all my life, Sienna," he murmured. "And I'm not finished loving you yet."

He kissed her then - not like the first time in Barcelona, or the last time before everything went wrong, but slow and certain, the kind that doesn't ask for a future because it already feels like one.

Her hands moved to his shoulders, and his settled at her waist. For a moment, the world stilled, as if the city itself leaned closer to listen.

When they finally drew apart, they stayed forehead to forehead, breathing the same quiet.
"Thank you," she said softly.
"For what?"
"For letting me arrive in my own time."
He smiled, eyes still closed. "I would've waited longer."

She looked at him, and it struck her how familiar peace could feel when you stop fighting it. He wasn't the boy from then, and she wasn't the girl who ran. They were something else now. Something built. She didn't know what tomorrow held, but for the first time, she wasn't afraid to open the door.

The second room hadn't been a mystery door or a metaphor wrapped in longing. This, here, now. This studio. This moment.

Sienna rested her chin on his shoulder and looked out at the skyline. The rooftops, the windows, all the second chances people didn't know they were still allowed.
A shared stillness, the kind you can only have with someone who's seen the worst in you and stayed anyway.

"You keep climbing," he said quietly. "You stop sometimes. You hate the incline. But then you look out, and for a minute, it makes sense."
"Climbing sounds exhausting," she said.
"That's why you don't do it alone."
She smiled, tired and full. He looked around the room - bare floor, enormous photo.

They sat on the floor, backs against the wall, the photograph above
them catching the last of the afternoon sun.
Sienna reached for Nico's hand, their fingers finding each other easily.
"We should get a couch," he said.
She smiled. "Maybe tomorrow."
220

For now, the room was enough.
The city moved outside, but inside, they stayed.

Two people, finally at home.

Sometimes we try to curate our lives, to control the moment, predict
the outcomes and leave before anything gets broken.
Is it independence or is it fear?

We exit a room early, to stand by the door so we can't be asked to stay.
And then, if we're lucky, something makes us turn back.
We walk back in and say, I am here now. A face, a moment, a truth.

It's not about being brave. Bravery fades.
What lasts is clarity.
Know which rooms are yours. Know which doors you closed because
someone else touched the handle first and which ones still wait quietly,
unlocked.

Find the second room you've been circling all this time. The one that
kept its light on.

And when you finally walk through, without regret, the room meets you
halfway.

Step inside.
Stay awhile.

TSR

www.ingramcontent.com/pod-product-compliance
Lightning Source LLC
Chambersburg PA
CBHW040526170726
48295CB00012B/360